Evie and the
ANIMALS

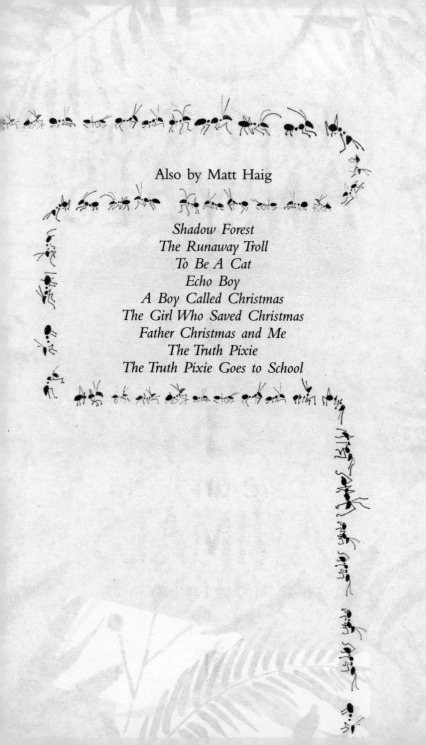

Also by Matt Haig

Shadow Forest
The Runaway Troll
To Be A Cat
Echo Boy
A Boy Called Christmas
The Girl Who Saved Christmas
Father Christmas and Me
The Truth Pixie
The Truth Pixie Goes to School

Matt Haig

Evie and the
ANIMALS

Illustrated by Emily Gravett

CANONGATE

This paperback edition published in 2020 by Canongate Books

First published in Great Britain in 2019 by Canongate Books Ltd,
14 High Street, Edinburgh EH1 1TE

canongate.co.uk

1

British Library Cataloguing-in-Publication Data
A catalogue record for this book is available on
request from the British Library

ISBN 978 1 78689 431 1

Typeset in Bembo by
Palimpsest Book Production Ltd, Falkirk, Stirlingshire

Printed and bound in Great Britain by Clays Ltd, Elcograf S.p.A.

MIX
Paper from
responsible sources
FSC® C018072

To Pearl and Lucas

And to all the children everywhere
trying to protect the earth and all
the glorious creatures who live here

'Some people talk to animals. Not many listen though. That is the problem.'
— A.A. Milne

A Special Child

Once there was a girl called Evie Trench.
Evie was not a normal child.
She was a 'special' child.
That's what her dad said.

Special.

Evie often thought it would be a lot easier to be a normal child than a special child, but there you go. She was *special*.

And the reason for this was . . .

Well, it was complicated. Evie didn't really understand it herself.

Before we get on to her specialness, let's start with a simple fact.

Evie liked animals. Of course, lots of people like animals. But Evie liked *all* animals. Not just the cuddly ones.

She liked dogs and cats, yes, of course, but also cockroaches, snakes, bats, vultures, hyenas, sharks, jellyfish and green anaconda snakes. She liked every animal. Well, apart from the Brazilian wandering spider – the deadliest spider in the world – which even Evie found hard to love, for reasons that will become clear. But, as a general rule, if it lived, she liked it.

And she knew everything about the animal world. As much as anyone. There were probably professors of Animal Biology at extremely clever universities who knew less than her. By the time she was six years old she had read more than three hundred books on the subject.

Every time she felt worried or sad or bored she would sit and read a book about animals.

So she knew *a lot*.

For instance, she knew that:

1. Snails can sleep for three years in a row and slugs have four noses.

2. A grizzly bear is so strong it can crush a bowling ball.
3. Birds don't find chilli peppers spicy.
4. All clownfish are born boys. (Some turn into girl clownfish later on.)
5. Cats can drink seawater with no problem.
6. An octopus has three hearts.
7. A reindeer's eyes turn blue in winter to help them see in the dark.
8. Elephants are pregnant for nearly two years.
9. Underneath their striped fur, tigers have striped *skin*.

And, her favourite:

10. Sea otters hold hands in their sleep so they don't drift away from each other.

But Evie didn't just *like* animals. She didn't just know *facts* about them.

3

She also had a very special skill.

A very unusual skill. The skill was this:

She could **HEAR** what animals were thinking.

And sometimes she could get animals to hear what she was thinking.

Without moving her lips or making a sound, Evie could talk to animals.

Evie had no idea how or why she could hear animals. She just could. And, as she got older, it seemed to be happening more and more often. And it was the best thing ever. It was her very own secret superpower. She had only ever told one person she could do this. Her dad. And he'd said that she must never tell anyone about it. Ever.

'You are special, but being special can get you into lots of trouble. Hearing the things you hear can, well . . . it can lead to bad things. Very bad things,' he'd said. 'Trust me. You must never tell anyone. And, whatever you hear, you must never communicate with animals. Never talk back to them. You know, with your mind.'

So she didn't. And no one knew.

Or so she thought.

At least until the day of the rabbit.

4

A Bird Called Beak

The day of the rabbit began with a bird.

A sparrow, in fact.

The sparrow – a small, reddish-brown ordinary little house sparrow – was called Beak.

Evie had chatted with the sparrow before. Mind-chatted, not mouth-chatted. But it was still chatting.

The bird often came for the seeds Evie left on her windowsill. Evie secretly picked the seeds off the multi-seeded loaf of bread her dad liked to buy.

Evie couldn't always hear the thoughts of animals. Some days she didn't hear the thought of a single creature. But Beak was one of the easiest animals to understand. Not as easy as dogs, but then, no creatures were.

'You seem sad today, Evie,' Beak was thinking, nibbling on seeds, as Evie stared out of her window at the morning sky.

And then Evie showed Beak the photo of her mum she kept by the bed. 'I miss her, Beak.'

'I miss my mum too,' Beak said. Not with his beak, but with his mind. 'To be fair, I only knew her for a short time, but she seemed great.'

'I never knew mine either. I mean, I can't really remember her. I get all my information from Granny Flora. And Dad, of course. Though not as much as you'd think from him. Is that strange? To miss things you never really knew?'

'Not at all. I miss all my friends I haven't made yet. And I have thousands of friends already. We fly around together. But I am still new. Young. I have not lived through a winter yet. There will be many more friends I will make. And I miss them. Because I am sure they will be special.'

Evie tried not to feel sad. 'What's it like to fly, Beak?'

'It's the easiest thing in the world. If you have wings. It's like freedom. To be able to go up and down and side to side and anywhere you want, with the wind rushing through your feathers, eating whatever flying insects come your way. You would like it, Evie.'

'I think I would. Apart from the eating insects part.'

'There is nothing like being free to be

yourself,' Beak added. 'If you have wings, you might as well use them.'

'Hmm. So I hear.'

And it was at that moment that her dad knocked on her door and pushed it open a little. Beak's tiny head jerked around.

'Uh-oh,' thought Beak.

'Come on, Evie, you should be ready for school by now,' Evie's dad said as he peeked his head through the door. He noticed the open window and the sparrow flying off into the sky.

He also saw the seeds on the windowsill. 'Evie, what have I told you about taking seeds off the bread to feed the birds?'

'I'm sorry, Dad. It was just, if I'm not allowed a pet I . . .'

'You weren't trying to talk to that bird, were you? With your mind, I mean?'

'No,' Evie lied. She had to. Her dad had made it *very clear* that she should always ignore the voices of animals that entered her mind because they would lead to **VERY BAD THINGS**.

Though he didn't tell her what those bad things might be. Which was annoying. Especially as Evie really, really did want a pet. 'I wasn't talking to the bird.'

'Good,' her dad said. He seemed tired. He had been working late, repairing other people's furniture in the garage. Maybe he was missing Mum, too. It was hard to tell. Evie wished her dad was as easy to understand as a dog.

It was a wish she had often. If he could just turn into a dog for a little while . . . If he was a dog, then she would understand him. A big slobbery bloodhound. The thing with dogs is that they can't help but tell you things. A kind of talking, but not with their mouths the way humans talk. You don't even have to read their minds to realise they are talking all the time. Every wag, every bark, every whimper, every tilt of the head, every soft stare, every breath and every pant is a kind of talking. It is saying something. Humans aren't often like that. Maybe that is why humans need words. Maybe it is just too hard to understand each other without them.

And dads, in particular, are one of the most complicated types of animal in existence.

'Now,' he said. 'School.'

8

A Rabbit in Need

A few hours later, Evie was sitting next to her best friend, Leonora Brightside, in the canteen of Lofting Primary School.

Evie was eating her vegetable lasagne, listening to Leonora talk about her new puppy. It was a Maltese terrier called Bibi. She had a picture on her phone.

Leonora's parents were famous vloggers. Their channel – LIFE ON THE BRIGHTSIDE – had two million subscribers on YouTube. Leonora had been starring in their videos since literally the day she was born, as her birth was filmed for one of the most popular episodes, 'Our Little Girl', which had been viewed 17,637,239 times.

'Mum did some research and found that Maltese terriers are the cutest breed according to internet users and would get us more hits. My dad is highly allergic to dogs but Mum says that he'll just have to sneeze. And, anyway, Bibi isn't making him sneeze.'

Evie knew why, of course. 'They're hypoallergenic, because they don't molt.'

'Ah,' said Leonora, eating her packed lunch of sushi rolls. 'You should come around and see her! Tonight! You'll love her. I mean, you love all animals, I know. Even the ugly ones. Even cockroaches. So you're going to love Bibi. She is totally *adorbs*. You could even be in a video! If, you know, you sorted your hair out a bit.'

'What's wrong with my hair?'

'It's just a bit, you know, *dull*.'

'Is it? I just thought it was hair,' said Evie, who never really gave too much thought to her appearance. She was tall-ish, for an eleven-year-old, with a small-ish nose and wide-ish eyes. It was all very *ish*. But everyone always said she had a 'kind smile' or a 'wise smile', which she supposed was better than having an unkind or stupid smile. But anyway, the one thing she really was okay about was her brown(ish) hair, because it was exactly the same shade and straightness as her mum's in all the photos.

'Hahahahahaha,' laughed Leonora, taking filtered selfies of herself as a unicorn. A unicorn eating sushi. 'You are **FUNNY**, Evie. I love you so much. But don't worry, *it's what's on the*

inside that counts. That's what Jay, dad's fitness instructor, says. Mind you, he is a male model.'

Evie shrugged. She sometimes didn't have words for Leonora. Like Leonora's words were water and she had to hold her breath for a while and just wait for them to end. Evie occasionally wondered why she was friends with Leonora, as she always made her feel bad about herself.

After lunch, Evie wanted to be on her own. So she decided to go to the school library. She *loved* the school library because it had a very large collection of books about nature and wildlife and animals. She remembered she had a book to take back. And the book was the *Encyclopaedia of Endangered Species.*

She had read it from cover to cover in two days and had got cross when she'd found out about all the different types of tiger that were already extinct, and that all the other types were only just hanging on. She had got crosser when she had read about leatherback sea turtles – the largest type of sea turtle – nearly being extinct, because they had been around for 110 million years, since the dinosaurs. As modern human beings had only been in existence for

200,000 years – which was nowhere near even *one* million years – it seemed a bit cheeky of us – *rude*, even – to be endangering all these other animals who had got here first and had been doing perfectly okay without us. Well, that's what Evie thought.

So there she was, on her own, holding the encyclopaedia and walking through the school corridors towards the library, when she passed Kahlo.

Kahlo was the new school rabbit. She was named after the famous Mexican artist Frida Kahlo, for some strange reason. She lived in a hutch just outside the school secretary's office.

The only time she had heard Kahlo think something was yesterday when she had been with Leonora. The rabbit had been at her water bottle and Evie had heard her say, 'Oh no.' But because she'd been with Leonora Evie hadn't stopped to check if Kahlo was okay.

But now, Evie heard a thought again.

A voice, a whisper, a whine, a *something*.

Evie turned.

'There's another one,' thought Kahlo to herself. 'Walking straight past. Not a care in the world.'

Evie stopped.

'Oh, this is no good. They'll die without me.'

Evie stared intensely at the rabbit. She found that, rather than closing her eyes, if she stared intensely at a creature, it was more likely to hear her thoughts.

'Kahlo, what is the matter?' she asked silently, as a couple of boys in the year below walked past, nudging each other and giggling about why Evie was standing staring at a rabbit.

The rabbit didn't notice the question, so Evie thought it again. She even whispered it to herself to make sure the thought was precise and clear in her mind.

'Kahlo. What. Is. The. Matter?'

Kahlo looked up and made eye contact with Evie. She had a sweet but sad face, with ears that pressed against the roof of the hutch.

'You understand what's in my head?' thought-asked the rabbit.

'Yes.'

'I've never seen a human do that. Other animals, all the time . . . But a human? That must be rare.'

Evie knew that was the case. A cat had once told her that it was because humans were too arrogant – which was a bit rich, coming from a cat.

The rabbit pressed her grey-brown face against the wires of the hutch and pleaded with her dark, shining, desperate eyes.

'I am not meant to be here. I belong in the woods. I was taken from the Forest of Holes. I belong in the warren. I belong with my colony.'

'The Forest of Holes?'

'Yes. It's very near. I was stolen by Brenda.'

'Brenda? Who on earth is Brenda?'

'Brenda. Brenda Baxter.'

Evie smiled. 'Mrs Baxter's a Brenda? Amazing. Brenda Baxter.' But then she realised what Kahlo had just said. 'Mrs Baxter, the head teacher stole you from the wild?'

'Yup.'

'That's terrible! She wouldn't do something like that!'

'Well, it's true. Rabbits don't lie. I was kidnapped. She took me. And I need to go back. I've got all my family. I've still got my mum. Do you know what it's like to be away from your mum?'

Evie felt a deep, familiar sadness. 'More than anything,' she said.

'Please. She's only two hundred hops away. Hopping! How I miss hopping! But I can

14

hardly do a hop in here without bashing my head. You've got to help me. You're the only one who can hear me.'

Evie felt worried all of a sudden. She looked around. No one was there. 'How do you want me to help you?'

'You have to get me out of here.'

Rabbit World

'How would you like to be in here?' asked Kahlo. 'Lying on some straw, staring out through all these metal squares. Scratching against that stupid tube for my water bottle. Having hundreds of human fingers try to poke at you every day. Look at this place. Could you live here?'

'Probably not,' Evie said, with her mind, not even whispering it now but still being understood. It did seem like a particularly small hutch for such a large rabbit, now Evie thought about it.

'Please. You have to help . . .'

Evie gulped and panicked and thought about what her dad would say if she helped the school rabbit escape from a hutch. Even a tiny hutch like this one.

'I'm sorry,' she said.

She left the rabbit and ran towards the library. Until she was spotted by Mrs Baxter herself.

'No running in the corridor, Evie,' she said sharply.

Evie stopped. She turned around. She saw Mrs

Baxter's stern face. Her mouth as small as a cat's bottom. 'Mrs Baxter, um, can I ask you something?'

Mrs Baxter sighed. 'If you must.'

'Do you think it would be possible to build Kahlo, the rabbit, a new hutch?'

'She has a hutch,' snapped Mrs Baxter.

'I mean, a *bigger* hutch. So she can hop about more. It seems sad for a rabbit not to be able to hop around. We could do it as a . . . as a . . . *project*.'

'Kahlo is a rabbit. She will have the hutch she's been given. There will be no bigger hutch. There will be no Five Star Rabbit Hotel. There will be no hutch with a swimming pool.'

'I'm pretty sure rabbits don't want swimming p—'

Mrs Baxter flapped her hand, as if Evie was a fly at a picnic. 'Now, Evie, we have the school inspectors coming next week and I have some very important paperwork to do. Goodbye.'

So, Evie walked to the library.

She handed in the *Encyclopaedia of Endangered Species*. She then found a book called *Rabbit World*. It was a book of photographs. All of rabbits. On page ninety-three there was a photo of a rabbit that looked so much like Kahlo it *could actually have been Kahlo*. And it was running around on a hillside full of holes, with loads of other rabbits. And even though it was a photograph, and you can't read the thoughts inside a photograph, Evie felt very strongly that the rabbit in the picture was happy.

And then the bell rang, so she put the book back on the shelf and walked out of the library.

When she passed Kahlo, she felt her thoughts again. And this time she could really feel the sadness, as if it was her own. It made her whole body heavy. Evie felt she might start crying, right there in the school corridor. It was almost, for a moment, like she *was* the rabbit.

'Oh no,' whispered Evie to herself.

Evie knew, in that moment, that she had no choice. She knew that if she was squashed inside the too-small hutch she would want someone to help her.

She knew, in other words, that she was about to do something very stupid indeed.

'Please,' said Kahlo. 'You have to help me. I have to get out of here.'

So Evie waited for the young Year Twos to walk past her, then she went over to the hutch, unlocked its two latches and picked up Kahlo. She was heavier and warmer than Evie had imagined.

Evie's heart was beating fast. And so – she realised – was the rabbit's. If she got caught, she would be in the biggest trouble of her life. She would get expelled. Or worse.

Still carrying the rabbit, Evie ran out of school. She ran over the playground and placed Kahlo down on the grass. Kahlo, whiskers twitching, looked up at Evie.

'Thank you. Thank you! You will be known as the Human Who Is Good! Thank you! Thank you . . .'

'Go,' Evie said. 'Quick, before anyone sees.'

And Kahlo was quick. Evie watched her hop away, towards the wooden fence at the edge of the playing field. Beyond were farm fields to the left, full of cows and bulls. To the right was Lofting Wood. The Forest of Holes, as Kahlo had put it.

'Keep going,' urged Evie, hoping the thought would reach the rabbit, who was now quite a distance from her, bouncing home towards her warren. 'And don't stop until you get there.'

Evie headed back into school, hoping no one had seen what she had just done, she felt Kahlo's fading rabbity thought hop into her mind:

'If you ever need a favour, just ask.'

21

How Evie Fell Out with Leonora

Evie was in Leonora's ginormous living room.

Leonora had texted her mum, who had texted Leonora's dad, who had texted Evie's dad, who had texted back to say it was okay.

Evie hadn't wanted to spend the evening with Leonora, but Leonora made things happen even if you didn't want them to. Evie had been friends with Leonora all through primary school, but now they were in their final year before high school it was becoming clear that they didn't have *that much* in common. They'd been the best friends in the world. They'd loved the same things and even had a special handshake and everything. But now they never did the handshake. And Leonora liked videos about make-up, and Evie liked videos about hippos and box jellyfish and how to buy less plastic. But perhaps, Evie imagined, it was good to be with Leonora, who spoke so fast and so often it was quite hard to have any kind of thoughts around her, even worried ones. And besides, Leonora had a new puppy.

Puppies made everything better. That was science.

But Evie was still worried. No one had noticed the rabbit was missing until afternoon break. And then Mrs Baxter had called an emergency assembly and the last hour of the school day had seen everyone in the school searching the field.

Evie kept wishing she hadn't said anything to Mrs Baxter about the hutch. Because surely, that night, Mrs Baxter would realise. And then tomorrow she'd be called into the office. And then her dad would be crosser than he'd ever been.

And . . . and . . . and . . .

Evie tried to shake all the worries and ands out of her head as she sat on the spin chair between the electric piano and the 75-inch TV. Leonora's mum was upstairs doing yoga and her dad was out, and Leonora had told Evie to film her putting clothes on Bibi.

Indeed Bibi, the fluffy white terrier puppy, was currently being squeezed into a tiny ballet outfit. She was already in the black leotard and

23

next was the tutu. The puppy didn't like this, Evie knew. Even though Bibi wasn't putting up much of a struggle, the small soft puppy thoughts were entering Evie's mind: 'I hate it, I hate it, make it stop!'

'I don't think she likes this.'

'Evie, shut up, we're filming. She looks funny!'

'I just don't think she finds it funny.'

'How do you know? Dogs can't laugh. She might be laughing inside.'

'She's not laughing inside. She doesn't like it.'

And then Leonora grabbed the phone from her. The puppy ran away. 'What's the matter with you, Evie?'

'Nothing.'

'Well, you're not being very fun. You are being the exact opposite of fun. You are being a **BIG WORLD-RECORD BORE**. Mummy says I should only have positive people in my life. That's why she unfollowed four hundred

people on Instagram. And you are not very positive. You are *un*positive.'

Then she screwed up her nose and said, 'I can't help it if you never knew your mum and all that.'

Evie felt tears burn behind her eyes. It had been a very long day. 'What has my mum got to do with anything?'

'I just think maybe we shouldn't be friends any more.'

'Fine.'

'*Fine.*'

'Fine.'

And then Leonora said Evie should call her dad to come and pick her up. So she did. And Leonora said that the doorbell wasn't working properly at the moment, so maybe it was best if Evie waited outside on the bench in front of the house.

So Evie left the house and sat and waited for her dad to pick her up, feeling alone and friendless and worried that she was going to get caught for freeing Kahlo the rabbit.

Two boys from the high school walked by, passing a football between them.

Don't cry, Evie thought to herself. She looked to the sky and saw three distant birds, flying high above. Maybe one was Beak. The thought of Beak, having fun in the sky, made her feel a bit happier.

Evie looked down to her side and saw a dog.

The dog was the scruffiest-looking thing Evie had seen in her life. It was quite a tall dog, *far* taller than a Maltese terrier, and a *bit* taller than a Labrador, but with slightly longer, shaggier hair. It wasn't any breed Evie recognised. It was probably a mix of about three hundred breeds. The dog was dust brown with mucky off-white patches. It was scrawny, and dirty, and bits of leaves and other rubbish were hanging off it.

'I am hurt,' thought the dog.

The easiest animals in the world to understand were dogs. Way easier than Beak. Way easier than rabbits. Dogs were so easy to mind-read and mind-chat with that Evie found it bizarre that more people couldn't do it. In fact, dogs were *too* easy to understand. Evie just had to walk past a house that contained a dog and the thoughts of that creature would enter her mind.

But if Evie walked past a dog in the street, then its thoughts would be especially clear. A fast list of smells normally. '*Salty – sour – new*

26

wee – old wee – cat wee.' It could be quite exhausting, especially if Evie was trying to have a conversation with someone.

This particular scruffy dog was hobbling. Its front right paw didn't touch the ground as the dog walked.

'Hey, dog,' said Evie out loud. 'I can help you. Let's look at your paw. Please. I won't hurt you. Give me your paw.'

Then she said the same thing, but silently. Pressing the thought into the dog's mind.

The dog did as Evie said. She raised his paw. Evie had a look and saw there was something sticking out of it. A little black triangle of a thorn.

'I'm hurt,' said the dog.

'I know,' thought Evie, staring at the dog. 'What I am about to do might hurt a little, but you will feel better afterwards.'

And the dog's eyes seemed to sparkle at being understood.

The dog stayed still, and he didn't even flinch as Evie pulled out the thorn.

She let go of the dog's scruffy paw and it lowered to the ground.

'Thank you,' the dog said. 'I will be able to run again. Running is my favourite.'

27

Evie remembered that Beak had said the same thing about flying.

And Kahlo had seemed to think the same thing about hopping.

Maybe all animals had their own kinds of freedom.

Evie wondered what it would be for humans.

She looked at the shaggy dog and asked, 'Have you got an owner? A home? A name?'

'Scruff,' he said. 'That's what the woman says. The woman who feeds me the meat the humans don't want. At the place where they come and eat.'

'A restaurant?'

'I don't know. But that's what she calls me. I like it. Scruff.'

'Cool. Well, I'm Evie.' She said it aloud, as well as thinking it. Which made her feel a bit mad.

A ginger tabby cat was prowling along the street. It hissed at Scruff.

'Come on, Marmalade,' Scruff told the cat. 'We've been through this. I'm not going to hurt you.'

'I know that,' said Marmalade. 'I just don't like you. You trouble me. All dogs trouble me.'

'That's prejudice,' said Scruff. 'Plain and simple.'

The cat slipped under a parked car to watch Scruff from a distance.

Evie asked a thought-question: 'Why do dogs and cats hate each other if they understand each other?'

Scruff sighed a panted sigh. 'Understand each other? Cats and dogs? We do and we don't. A bit like humans and humans.'

A man walked past, carrying shopping from the supermarket. He glanced at Evie but didn't think anything weird was going on. It just looked like an eleven-year-old girl silently stroking a dog.

Then Evie saw her dad's car heading towards her.

29

'Where do you live, Scruff?' wondered Evie.

'Everywhere. And nowhere.'

'You don't have an owner?'

'Don't be ridiculous. I've got dignity. I'm a free agent.'

Scruff sniffed the ground. And did a wee against the bench.

'House dogs leave their scent everywhere. It's like they own the place. I have to keep on top of it. Let them know who really runs these streets. It's getting ridiculous.'

Evie's dad's small, battered, old green car pulled up at the kerb. 'That's my dad. I'd better go. But I'll see you around, Scruff.'

Evie stood up. Then the dog sniffed her. 'You smell of house dog. And rabbit. And fear.'

Evie sighed. 'Yeah. It's been a weird day.'

'And goodness. You've got goodness in you. You are good, Evie. Don't let that fade away. It sometimes does, you know, with humans.'

Evie walked to the car and looked up towards Leonora's bedroom.

'Yeah. It does. Bye, Scruff.'

'Okay. Sniff you later. Life is good.'

Life is good.

Evie wished she could feel the same. But right then, that's all life seemed to be: one wish after another. She wished she could remember her mum better. She wished best friends could stay being best friends. She wished her dad talked to her more. She wished she didn't have the knot of worry in her stomach about freeing Kahlo. But she *was* pleased that Scruff was no longer hurting.

The dog trotted happily away, enjoying his newly painless paw, and although she might have lost one friend that day, Evie felt she had also made a new one.

As she got into the car she was pleased to see her grandma, Granny Flora, sitting in the front seat. It was Wednesday. Of course. Granny Flora always came around for dinner on Wednesdays.

Granny Flora was the best granny in the world, but there was one thing Evie didn't know about her.

And she was about to find out.

Granny Flora's Big Secret

Granny Flora was eighty-one years old. She always had a twinkle in her eye and a bag of liquorice sweets in her cardigan pocket. She had a kind face, shaped like an egg, and as lined as a map. She smelled of lavender and wore tweed skirts and had a deep chuckly laugh that made you feel happy. And she liked to wink at you, just to let you know she was on your side.

She also had a pet bearded dragon called Plato. Evie had tried many times to read the thoughts of Plato but had never been able to.

Anyway, Plato went everywhere with Granny Flora.

She was even there now, by Granny Flora's ankles, eating some raw cabbage from a saucer in the middle of Evie's living room.

Evie's dad was also there. Scratching his beard. Staring at his phone. 'Sorry, but I'm going to have to repair a sofa in the garage. The people want to pick it up tomorrow.'

Granny Flora looked at him sharply. 'I am starting to think if we want to spend time with you we should maybe turn ourselves into a broken piece of furniture!'

'Not funny,' said Evie's dad, with a slight smile.

'Sofas don't ever ask you how you are feeling,' said Granny Flora. 'I suppose that's why you like them.'

'Maybe that's it.'

Granny Flora winked at Evie. 'Don't mind us,' she said. 'Me and Evie will find something to talk about, I'm sure.'

And then as soon as Evie's dad had shuffled out of the room, Granny Flora gave Evie a liquorice and leaned back in her chair and smiled a strange smile.

'It's getting stronger, isn't it?' she said.

Evie was confused. 'What is?'

'The Talent.'

'What talent?'

Granny Flora chuckled. 'That's what it's called, buttercup. The Talent. You know, the ability you have. The ability to communicate with animals. Telepathically. Most animals have it instinctively. They are connected to the natural world. But very few humans have it. Not these days. Only the special ones. Like you. Like your mother. And like me.'

Evie gasped. The words clogged her brain. This was **TOO MUCH INFORMATION**.

She didn't know what to say. She had never admitted to any human, apart from her dad, what she could do. She had felt like a complete weirdo. Why hadn't her dad told her about her mum and Granny Flora?

She knew her mum had loved animals. That's why she had gone on a trip to the Amazon rainforest for a month. To try to protect the rainforest and the endangered animals that lived there and the **WHOLE PLANET** from the people who were destroying it. And that's where she had died. She had been bitten on the ankle by a Brazilian wandering spider, the world's deadliest spider. The one and only type of animal that Evie found hard to love.

Evie had a million questions. But all she found herself asking was: 'How did you know about me?'

Granny Flora stared down at the brown–green reptile at her feet.

34

'Plato told me . . . He knows everything. You won't be able to understand him yet, because these are complicated creatures. But they know a lot about the world. They see everything. Past, present, sometimes even future. And bearded dragons are the wisest of the wise . . . Oh, and someone else hinted too.'

'Dad?' Evie wondered.

'No. A little birdy.'

'Beak!'

Granny Flora laughed softly. 'Yes. He'll tell you anything for a handful of crumbs, won't he?'

'Wow,' said Evie, thinking aloud. 'I'm not a freak! I'm like you! And Mum was like this too . . .'

Granny Flora's face grew serious, like a sky filling with clouds. 'You must know

that the Talent is not a blessing. It is a curse. It took over my life. It took over your mother's life.'

'But Mum did great things.'

'Yes. And in her, the Talent grew very strong. She could communicate with every animal. Every fish, every bird, every reptile. And animals loved her. But it led her too far. She should never have gone to the rainforest.'

Evie was confused. 'I don't understand something. If she was so good at talking to animals, why was she killed by one?'

Granny Flora looked around her suddenly. As if someone might be listening in. 'You are just like your mother. Asking questions about things that you wouldn't want to know the answer to.'

'But—'

Granny Flora pressed a finger to her own lips. 'Please, Evie. Listen. I know about what happened today. With the rabbit.'

'How?'

And Evie noticed Plato was staring straight at her with his small, round eyes. Evie felt a strange weak feeling as she looked at the lizard. She couldn't hear the lizard's mind, but she could sense his power. And it was quite scary.

'As I said,' said Granny Flora, popping a liquorice into her mouth. 'Plato knows *everything*.'

'Please don't tell Dad.'

'I won't. But he is going to find out.'

Evie felt fear chill her skin.

'And that would only be the start of the trouble. Please, you must try to keep the Talent under control. You must never act on it.'

'But why?'

'The more you act on it, the stronger it becomes. You are eleven now. That's when it really kicked in for me. Eleven, twelve, thirteen. Every year it grew stronger because I kept concentrating on all the animals. I'd lie on the grass and hear the stressed-out thoughts of marching ants. I'd re-live the nightmares of mice underneath the floorboards. I'd see a flock of birds and their thoughts would be so sudden that all at once I'd faint on the spot. It drove me mad for a while because I kept talking back. You know, silently, in my head. I kept having those conversations. I wanted to understand every animal that ever lived. And eventually, trust me, trouble will look for you. Like it did for me . . . Which is why I ended up in prison.'

Evie gasped. 'Prison?'

Granny Flora frowned. 'Oh yes. When I was twenty-one years old I went to prison. I have never told anyone this story until now. Are you ready to listen?'

Evie nodded. And secretly hoped Granny Flora hadn't gone to prison because of a rabbit.

Why Granny Flora Went to Prison

A lot of people who go to prison are there because they have burgled a house or shot somebody or stolen an expensive diamond. But Granny Flora had done nothing like that.

Granny Flora had been a good person.

Evie knew this because Granny Flora told her.

'I was a good person,' she said.

But she had got into big trouble for releasing all the animals at Mr Bullwhip's Travelling Circus back in the olden days.

'They kept elephants in chains, and elephants don't like being in chains. Nor do tigers or zebras. In fact, no one does,' Granny Flora explained.

'Tigers?' asked Evie.

Granny Flora looked a bit sheepish. 'Yes. That's why I went to prison. Because I released the tigers. They weren't bothered about the

39

zebras, though they were private property. And they weren't *too* bothered about the elephants – though they should have been, because elephants can be very grumpy indeed. No. They were mainly bothered about the tigers. And, to be fair, they prowled around Lofting town centre and everyone was scared. Two of them even went into the supermarket.'

Evie thought about this for a while. 'Well, I suppose they were tigers. So they could have eaten people.'

Granny Flora shook her head a little crossly. 'Not these tigers. They had promised.'

Evie was confused. 'Promised?'

'Yes. Promised. And tigers are many, many things. But one thing they are not are breakers of a promise. A tiger *always* keeps a promise.'

'How did you make them promise?'

'Well, buttercup, I asked them. Very politely. You have to be polite with tigers. That's what people don't understand. In fact, "I told them it was a condition. I said: "I will only release you from your chains if you absolutely promise not to eat anybody."''

'And what did they say?'

'They considered it very carefully and then said, "What, not even Mr Bullwhip, the circus

40

owner who is nasty to us every day and who looks extremely tasty?" and I said, "No. Not even nasty Mr Bullwhip. I am sure he is tasty, but no. It's a matter of principle." And they growled and grumbled a little but eventually they agreed. And you know what?'

Evie didn't know what, so she said: 'What?'

'They kept their promise.' She smiled sadly. 'But the police and the judge and everyone else laughed at me when I told them this. They thought I was joking. And then they locked me away for years. And . . . and . . . and . . .'

Granny Flora pulled a crumpled handkerchief from the inside sleeve of her cardigan and wiped her eyes with it. 'And . . . I was at rock bottom. But, well, the important thing about rock bottom is the rock part. You know you have something solid inside you. Something

that can't be smashed any further. The unbreakable part. And you are tough, Evie. I can tell. And you are clever. But sometimes in life it's best not to be *too* clever. Being *too* clever gets you into all kinds of trouble. There are some things you are better off not knowing. And some voices you are better off not hearing. So please, no more. Please, don't end up like I did. Don't end up like your mother. You can have a normal life.'

A normal life.

Evie nodded and tried to agree. But she realised, right then, that being special was who she was. She doubted, really, that she would ever have a normal life.

And, of course, she was absolutely right.

The Snake and the Frog

That night Evie had a dream.

The dream wasn't about a rabbit. It wasn't even about Granny Flora or a circus or a prison. It was about a snake.

A tree snake.

A tree snake on one of those low, twisty trees that you find deep in the jungle.

It wasn't an anaconda, because it wasn't in or around a river. But it was green. Bright green. It was a bright green emerald tree boa. Evie knew that. She knew that it could kill, not with venom but by crushing or, if its prey was small enough, biting.

And it had spotted something on the ground.

A frog. This frog was also brightly coloured. It was bright blue and black. It was the prettiest frog ever. It was a poison dart frog. Evie had read that they contained more poison than the Brazilian wandering spider, so were arguably the deadliest creature in the whole Amazon. She knew that they wouldn't

43

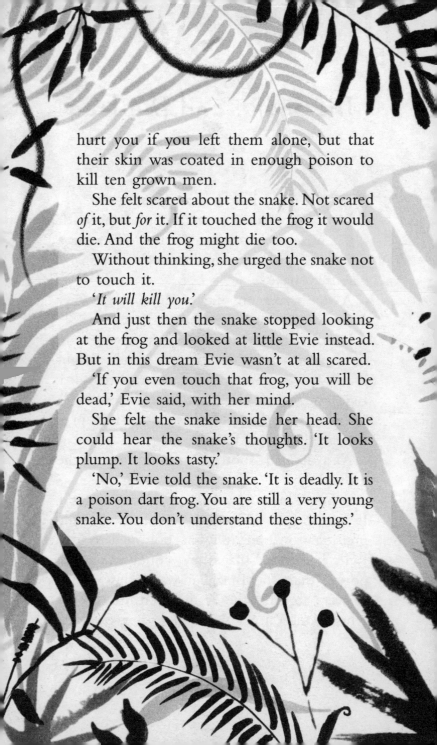

hurt you if you left them alone, but that their skin was coated in enough poison to kill ten grown men.

She felt scared about the snake. Not scared *of* it, but *for* it. If it touched the frog it would die. And the frog might die too.

Without thinking, she urged the snake not to touch it.

'*It will kill you.*'

And just then the snake stopped looking at the frog and looked at little Evie instead. But in this dream Evie wasn't at all scared.

'If you even touch that frog, you will be dead,' Evie said, with her mind.

She felt the snake inside her head. She could hear the snake's thoughts. 'It looks plump. It looks tasty.'

'No,' Evie told the snake. 'It is deadly. It is a poison dart frog. You are still a very young snake. You don't understand these things.'

The snake was confused. 'Why do you want to save me?'

Even in a dream Evie found this an easy question to answer. 'Because I can.'

She knew that both the snake and the frog could kill her, but that didn't mean she wanted them dead.

'Thank you,' thought the snake. 'You are a good human. Not like Mortimer.'

'Mortimer?'

'He is after me. He is trying to control me. He is not like you. Or your parents.'

Evie watched the poison dart frog hop away underneath a log. Then she turned her attention back to the snake. 'You know my parents?'

'Yes, they are right there.'

And the tree snake slid back up the tree and out of her thoughts and, in the dream, Evie turned around and saw her parents. She was the height of a toddler in this dream, so they towered above her. Her dad looked younger and happier and he had no beard. And her mum looked as kind and warm as she did in the photo.

'Mum!' she said. And she tried to hug her. But that was where the dream ended.

46

When she woke up, she had a very weird feeling.

As though the dream hadn't really been a dream at all.

It had felt, in fact, like a memory.

A Meeting with Mrs Baxter

Mrs Baxter sat behind her desk. On her wall there was a poster that said, 'The soul is healed by being with children', which was, according to the poster, a quote by someone called Fyodor Dostoyevsky.

Mrs Baxter didn't look very healed right now. She looked cross. And shocked. As if she had never in her whole life been confronted with a naughtier child.

She was dipping a teabag into her tea. She kept bobbing it up and down.

'It's chamomile,' she explained, in a reassuringly calm voice. 'Chamomile tea. It says it calms people down. I need calming down. This is my seventeenth of the day.'

Evie smiled. And felt nervous. And didn't know what to say.

'Evie Trench, Evie Trench, Evie Trench . . .'

Evie had been called into Mrs Baxter's office in the middle of a lesson (on Vikings), so she

48

knew it was serious. Of course it was serious. She knew what this was about.

'So, you have something to tell me . . .'

'Um, do I?' asked Evie, nervously.

'We have cameras everywhere in this school. We know you stole Kahlo.'

'I . . . I didn't steal her.'

'Well, what would you call it then?'

Evie fished for the word. 'Rescued. I rescued her. The hutch was too small. She wanted to escape.'

Mrs Baxter's face grew redder and redder. She was a giant tomato of anger.

'Do not try to correct me in my own office.' She took a deep breath. 'Now, there is no excuse for endangering the health and welfare of an animal.'

'I'm really sorry, Mrs Baxter, but I was actually doing the opposite. Kahlo hated being in that hutch. She wanted to be free. She wanted to escape back to where she was from.'

Mrs Baxter was staring at Evie with wide,

disbelieving eyes. 'Oh, and how do you know this? Are you a rabbit mind-reader or something?'

Evie panicked. 'No. Of course not. No. That would be . . . *impossible*. It's just I imagined that she must be feeling squished up.'

Mrs Baxter started rubbing her temples. Then she rummaged in her desk drawer. 'Headache pills . . . headache pills . . .' She found the headache pills and swallowed two at once. She drank the remains of her tea in a big gulp.

'I was so nearly an actor, you know?' she said. 'I came *this close*. I could be playing Titania in *A Midsummer Night's Dream* for the Royal Shakespeare Company right now. But no, here I am, in Lofting, dealing with an eleven-year-old rabbit thief.'

'I don't have the rabbit.'

There was a knock at the door. 'Well, maybe your father will be able to help.'

'No. Please. Don't call my dad. I beg you.'

Mrs Baxter smiled an evil grin. 'Too late.'

The door opened and Evie saw her dad, looking pale and serious, and Evie wished she could disappear into the ground. Like a rabbit.

'I am so sorry about Evie's behaviour, Mrs Baxter,' her dad said, taking a chair beside Evie. 'This has never happened before. And this will never happen again. I assure you. I can see, Mrs Baxter, this is not the way of things here, nor should it be. You are an exceptional head teacher.'

'You are right, Mr Trench. In the entire history of Lofting Primary School, no one has ever stolen a rabbit. And it won't happen again because we can't afford to keep buying rabbits for them to be stolen.'

Evie really knew she should stay quiet, but she couldn't help it. 'I didn't steal it, Dad. I released it.'

Her dad stared at her. And said, in a quiet but incredibly stern voice, 'Evie, it doesn't matter whether it was stealing or releasing. You took it. It was an incredibly stupid thing to do.'

And then he turned to Mrs Baxter. 'I am so sorry for my daughter's behaviour. I will obviously pay however much you paid for the rabbit and I assure you Evie will be suitably punished. I will make her write "I MUST NEVER TAKE A RABBIT OUT OF ITS HUTCH EVER EVER AGAIN" a thousand times on a piece of paper. And no pocket money. For . . . a year.'

Evie's mouth dropped open in disbelief. She wondered what was going through her dad's mind. She knew she would be in a *bit* of trouble, but she had never seen her dad act like this.

Mrs Baxter was quite impressed by this display of parental crossness.

'Well, I can see, Mr Trench, that you understand the seriousness of this matter.'

'I do. I absolutely do. You don't have to worry at all, Mrs Baxter.'

'I'm not sure it's as simple as that . . . You see, there is a school inspection next week and the subject of the rabbit is bound to come up. And we need to look tough. And so I really think Evie will have to find somewhere else to get her schooling.'

Evie's dad looked like he could cry. 'You're expelling her?'

'I see no other option.'

A memory popped into Evie's mind. 'Erm,' she said, 'do you think the school inspectors would be interested to know where you got the rabbit from?'

Now it was Mrs Baxter's turn to look worried. 'What are you talking about?'

Evie's heart raced. She knew it would make her dad sad and cross if she got expelled, so she had to do something. She tried to keep her voice calm. 'There were witnesses who saw you take the rabbit from the forest. A head teacher should not be stealing wild rabbits.' Evie didn't add that the witnesses were all rabbits because that might have spoiled the story.

Mrs Baxter looked furious but was totally lost for words. 'I . . . I . . . do you have *any idea* how hard it is to balance the school budget? I have to make cuts somewhere!'

'Well,' Evie said. 'Maybe you'll explain that to the inspectors.'

'Or . . .' interrupted her dad. 'We could just all forget this ever happened.'

There was a long silence. Mrs Baxter stared at Evie. Evie's dad stared at Evie. And Evie stared at her shoes.

Eventually Mrs Baxter spoke.

'Good, good. Well, in that case, no further action is required by myself or the school.'

Evie's dad smiled, gratefully. 'Thank you, Mrs Baxter. Say "thank you", Evie. And that you are grateful to Mrs Baxter for her kindness.'

Evie squeezed out a 'thank you'. The most difficult thank you of her life.

Then Mr Trench looked directly into the head teacher's stern-but-softening eyes and said what he was planning to say all along.

'May I ask you something, Mrs Baxter?'

'Of course.'

'Well, I was just wondering if we could make sure no one else knows about this? I am just thinking of your school. I mean, you have such a great reputation. And I'd hate for that to change.'

Mrs Baxter took a deep breath, as if inhaling what had just been said. 'You are right. We mustn't say another word about this. It would lead to the wrong kind of questions. But any more trouble like this and you will have to take your problematic offspring elsewhere. You understand?'

Evie watched her father smile and stand up and – almost – *bow* in front of Mrs Baxter. 'One hundred per cent,' he said, just as the bell went. Then he put on his cross voice. 'Now, come on, Evie, let's take you home.'

The Name from the Dream

In the car, Evie tried to work out her dad's level of crossness. He was definitely a *bit* cross. But maybe not as cross as he had been showing Mrs Baxter.

'I am not cross, Evie. I am sad that you can't keep the one secret I asked you to keep.'

Evie stared out at moving trees. 'I was helping a rabbit. Rabbits are people, too. Not humans, but still people. They have feelings. They are intelligent. They—'

'You promised you weren't going to do this.'

There was a long silence.

'I know. I'm sorry. I know.'

They passed a messy-looking dog sniffing a lamp-post. It was Scruff. But the car was going too fast for any of his thoughts to enter Evie's mind.

'I've told you,' her dad was saying. 'You mustn't do this. If you start *listening* to animals, it will lead to big trouble . . .'

55

Evie nodded. She assumed he was talking about what Granny Flora had been talking about. About how the voices of all the animal thoughts end up driving you mad. But then he said something under his breath. A word – or a name – that froze her with terror.

'*Mortimer.*'

Mortimer. Evie had heard that name somewhere. And then she remembered, as her heart began to race.

The dream!

The dream of the tree snake and the poison dart frog.

The tree snake had mentioned him.

Evie was troubled. She was scared of asking the question she knew she had to ask. 'Who is *Mortimer*, Dad?'

As the car chugged onto Lofting Road, Evie's dad started to mumble to himself. She stared at her dad's face. He looked tired. His eyes had bags under them and the bags themselves had more bags under them. Dads were mysteries.

Evie couldn't hear the words he was mumbling, or not all of them. But he did seem to be asking himself something. And the words 'now is the time' came out of his mouth.

He turned to his daughter and said, 'Evie, I

56

was going to wait until you were sixteen, but there is something you need to know. First, I need to show you something.'

Evie gulped. 'Is this about Mum?'

'Yes. It's about Mum. It's about us. It's about everything.' He parked the car and shakily ran his fingers through his thinning hair. 'Okay,' he said. 'Follow me.'

Evie saw a squirrel on a branch on the tree near the house. Evie knew this squirrel. She had often talked with it.

'Why are you sad?' the squirrel asked. 'Have you run out of nuts?'

Evie just walked on, ignoring her, as she followed her dad.

The Girl from the Jungle

They were in the garage. It smelled of damp and seemed, suddenly, full of secrets. They were standing there surrounded by broken chairs and sofas that Evie's dad was in the middle of repairing, all with the stuffing leaking out of them.

Evie held the piece of paper her dad had just given her. At the top of the document were the words 'Acta de Nacimiento'.

It was a birth certificate.

Evie's hands were shaking.

The name on it was 'Isabella Eva Navarro'.

'Who is this?' Evie asked.

And then she saw that the birth date was her own birthday.

But the place of birth was not London, as she'd always been told. It said 'Tena, Ecuador'.

'What is this?' she asked, her mouth dry with worry. 'Who is this?'

But, of course, even as the questions came out of her mouth, she was sensing the answer.

58

Her dad rubbed his tired eyes. 'You might need to sit down.'

Evie plonked herself on one of the broken sofas.

He was speaking calmly now, as if he was talking about something he'd forgotten to get in the supermarket. 'You weren't born in England, Evie. You were born in the city of Tena in Ecuador. In the Amazon rainforest. You moved here when you were three years old. I told you your old life was one big dream. That it never happened. And, eventually, you forgot about where you were when you were three.'

Evie felt her breathing go funny.

'Is . . . is this a joke?'

But her dad's face had never looked more serious. 'You were called Isabella Eva. Isabella was my mother's name. She died when I was a boy, still at school in Madrid.'

This was getting weirder and weirder.

'Madrid?'

'I was born in Spain. My mother was English and my father was Spanish.'

'Dad, do you speak Spanish?'

'Yeah. It is my first language, but we often spoke English at home when I was little. I am bilingual. My original job was a translator. And

59

I stayed being a translator when I moved to Ecuador. That is how I met your mum. She was already over there, trying to save the rainforest. Trying to save the animals.'

Evie looked at her dad as if a stranger had taken over his body.

'Eva was your middle name. Mum always called you Evie, so that was your new name when we moved here. And Trench. Trench was our new surname. And I changed my first name from Santiago to Leo.'

Evie stared at her dad in total disbelief. It felt so strange. As if she wasn't real. 'You changed our names! I don't understand.'

Evie's voice was getting cross and now her dad had a tear in his eye. 'I'm sorry, Evie. I had to do it. I had to do it for you. I had to do it for your mother. I had made her a promise. To keep you safe. We had to start again. New names. New country. New *everything*.'

Evie couldn't believe it. 'Am I Evie or am I Isabella?'

'You are Evie. You are Evie Trench. It's just . . . You didn't start off that way.'

Evie had ten thousand questions, but they all came down to one. She peered into her father's eyes. 'Why?'

'Your mum was a very special woman,' he said. 'Even more special than I have told you. She was like you. A good human to her very bones. She wanted to save the rainforest – the Amazon rainforest – from being destroyed. And that is why she went to South America. Not for a month, like I told you. She lived there for eleven years. Including the three years you were there too. Mostly in the city. But sometimes in a hut right in the jungle.'

Evie thought again of her dream. The snake and the frog. It now seemed that it wasn't a dream at all.

'Are you okay?' her dad said. 'Shall I keep going? Shall I tell you everything?'

Evie nodded in a daze. She couldn't believe there was still more to find out. She stared down at the birth certificate in her trembling hands.

'Your mum had the Talent, Evie. Animal telepathy. Just like you, and she was hearing all the animals. The animals told her terrible stories about the humans who were destroying their land. And she helped them. She told the animals what was happening and where to hide. She was a hero to the people who wanted to save the rainforest. But other people didn't like her.

The business people. The loggers. The cow farmers. And one man in particular *really* didn't like her.'

Evie was wondering – dreading – what was going to come next. She felt every inch of her skin wake up, the hairs standing on end, as if her whole body was listening.

'You see,' her dad continued. 'She could get inside the mind of any animal. The most weird and wonderful animals you ever saw. Macaws, squirrel monkeys, sloths, jaguars . . . Creatures that seemed like they were from another world. But she wasn't the only one out there with the Talent. There was someone else. Someone even more powerful than your mum.'

'Mortimer,' whispered Evie.

Her dad nodded. 'That's right. Mortimer J Mortimer. The worst man ever to have lived.'

Mortimer J Mortimer

'Mortimer J Mortimer,' said Evie's dad, 'was — and is — the most terrifying human monster.'

Evie hugged her knees into her chest, frightened. 'Who is he?'

Evie's dad clicked on his phone and showed Evie a picture of a man in a jungle. A man with a black moustache and a snake around his neck and a devilish smile. He had his arms folded and some kind of tattoo on his right hand.

'He is a robber and a killer,' Evie's dad explained. 'He uses his powers for evil. Powers so strong he doesn't just communicate with animals; he can actually take over their minds. He can control them. And that's what he did. Sometimes he would simply take an exotic animal and sell it. Or he'd take over the mind of a monkey and get the monkey into tents or huts in the jungle to steal whatever was there. He once used an anaconda snake to help him rob people on a jungle cruise. And that wasn't the worst of it. Sometimes Mortimer J Mortimer would get paid by companies clearing the forest for farmland to "silence" the people trying to save the forest. They didn't know about the Talent. They just knew he could make problems, and people, disappear. He kept a matchbox full of bullet ants – as you probably know, the deadliest ants in the world – and would tell them to bite whoever was getting in the way of business.'

Evie gulped. It felt as if she was listening to a horror story. But a real life one.

'He was looking for people to join him. Especially those who had the Talent. So they could use their powers together to take over the world.'

Evie's head ached from how weird this all was.

'He wanted Mum?' Evie asked.

Her dad nodded, and scratched his beard nervously. 'People like your mum. People like . . . *you*.'

He told Evie how Mortimer had found out from a scarlet macaw about the rumours that there was a woman somewhere else in the jungle – far away – who could communicate with animals. And how Mortimer had travelled thousands of miles down the Amazon river, from Brazil to Ecuador, to find her. To ask her to join him. He promised Evie's mum money. Lots of money. More money than she could ever have dreamed of.

Of course, Evie's mum said no.

'He noticed something. He was weakening around her. He thought she was weakening his powers, just by being alive. By having a Talent that she used for good. That's what he said to her. That's what she told me on that last night . . .' A tear slipped down Evie's dad's cheek. He wiped it away with the back of his hand.

'The next day he took control of a Brazilian wandering spider and . . .' He sniffed and looked into space. 'I tried everything to save her, but we were too far from a hospital. And your mum knew you were in danger too. I don't know if the animals had told her, but she said he would be

after you if he ever found out you had the Talent. So that is why we disappeared. After your mum died from the spider's venom we came to England, to be near Granny Flora, and asked her to move too, just to be safe.'

Evie closed her eyes, as if the dark would help her understand all this. 'Why didn't you tell me before?'

'I'll show you,' her dad said.

He stood up, went over to the same rusty filing cabinet where he'd got the birth certificate from and found some old newspaper cuttings from local newspapers.

Evie flicked through them, looking at the headlines and the photos next to them.

MAN, 29, DIES FROM SHARK BITE IN QUEENSLAND, AUSTRALIA

WOMAN KILLED BY SWARM OF BEES

TEENAGER EATEN BY PIRANHAS

'And do you know what all those people had in common?'

Evie shrugged. 'Bad luck?' she asked hopefully.

Her dad sighed. 'Unfortunately not. They all had the Talent. Every one of them.'

He showed her more newspaper clippings. She saw that the photo of the man who was killed by a shark had been in the paper a month before under the headline **'LOCAL MAN CLAIMS HE CAN TALK TO ANIMALS'**. And the same with the woman. (**'THE WOMAN WHO UNDERSTANDS WHAT BEES ARE SAYING.'**) And the teenager. (**'I CAN TALK TO MY DOG AND HE TELLS ME HE LIKES LISTENING TO BEYONCÉ.'**)

68

Evie's dad was now pacing in circles around a chair with a broken arm rest. 'Evie, this is why I had to make sure Mrs Baxter wasn't going to publicise what happened with the rabbit! This is why you have to keep it secret! Mortimer uses animals to kill everyone with the Talent. This is why you must *never* act on it again. Do you understand?' Her dad's face suddenly softened, as if a storm cloud had passed by and the sun had come out.

'I understand. I won't any more,' Evie said sadly. 'From now on. I'll ignore all the thoughts of animals.'

And she meant that promise. She really did.

69

One year later . . .

The New Reality

It was breakfast time. Evie's dad put on some music while making himself peanut butter on toast. Evie's dad *lived* on peanut butter. Peanut butter on toast for breakfast. Peanut butter sandwich for lunch. Evie was pretty sure he would have even had peanut butter for dinner if he could have got away with it.

'I've switched brands,' he told her. 'This is called Sun Crunch Peanut Butter. No palm oil! For the orangutans. And no plastic. For the fish.'

'Yay!' said Evie. 'The fish and the orangutans are very grateful, I imagine.'

The music was an old Spanish song called '*Esta Tarde Vi Llover*'. It meant something like 'This Afternoon I Watched the Rain'. It was a very old-fashioned song, apparently one Evie's dad had listened to as a child in Madrid, and Evie liked it. She understood some of the words because her dad was now teaching her Spanish.

Talking in Spanish was nowhere near as good as talking to animals, but at least Evie and her dad were getting on a bit better. And Spanish was quite cool. She liked that if you asked a question in Spanish, it started with an upside down question mark. So if you wanted to say 'What does that mean?' in Spanish, it was '*¿Qué significa eso?*'

Her dad had seemed a bit happier since he had told Evie the truth. A bit lighter. He was also looking healthier. Evie had insisted he drive less and ride a bike instead, after lecturing him on carbon emissions and polluted air. ('You sound just like your mum,' he told her. 'She would be so proud of you.') But there were still worries. She could feel them when she passed him sometimes. It was like walking through a cloud.

So she tried to make him feel less worried.

Evie kept hearing the thoughts of animals. Of course she still *heard* animals. When she walked past a dog or a cat she would often pick up their thoughts. But she had learned to ignore them.

She still *cared* for animals. She still *worried* about endangered animals. She still *read* about animals. She still *loved* animals. And, like her mum had been, she was dedicated to saving wildlife and the environment.

She told anyone who would listen about how the Amazon rainforest was the 'lungs of the earth' because it provided a fifth of the world's oxygen and it shouldn't be destroyed. And about the importance of having super-short showers. And how mountain gorillas had been saved from the brink of extinction by conservationists. Or about how melting Arctic sea ice meant that polar bears were in great danger. Or how sea turtles had far more girl babies than boy babies now because of rising temperatures.

But she stayed away from direct contact with animals.

For instance, she had left seeds out on her windowsill that morning for Beak but, as she did nowadays, had quickly ran out of the bedroom so that Beak wouldn't try to talk to her.

And slowly, sadly, she had noticed that she was starting to walk past many animals without reading their minds at all. Granny Flora had said the more you act on the Talent, the stronger it becomes. Well, the opposite was also true. The less you acted on it, the weaker it became. Maybe in a few years' time it would be gone forever.

Which meant she would be safe from Mortimer J Mortimer.

74

Evie was destined for a very safe and very boring life.

She tried to imagine what life had been like when she was a girl called Isabella living in Ecuador. In the rainforest.

But it was hard.

After all, Lofting was very different to a rainforest.

Sure, there was rain. But the dribbly kind, not the intense jungle kind.

Lofting was cold. And there weren't that many trees. And instead of huts there were houses made of orange bricks. And the sky was grey. And there was a big church that was also grey that had a steeple like a witch's hat. And there were no spider monkeys or glass frogs or jaguars or parrots or piranhas.

She told no one the truth about where she was born, or her original name. The past was so far away it might as well not have existed.

But she did keep having that same dream. The whole year that had passed since the rabbit incident had been one of weird sleep. In fact, now she was at her new school – 'big school', as Granny Flora called it – she'd been having the dream a lot more. The one about the tree snake and the poison dart frog. And, over her morning toast and peanut butter, she said to her dad: 'I had that dream again. The one where I could mind-read a tree snake and I saved it from a poisonous frog. I could communicate with it *telepathically* and it felt very, very real. I think it might have happened.'

Her dad stopped looking at his phone and sipped his coffee and said, 'Well, that sounds like a very interesting dream.'

Evie stared at him. 'But that's what I'm saying. It doesn't feel like *just* a dream. It feels like a *memory* that happens in a dream. It feels like something that happened.'

Her dad was shaking his head. 'The thing is, Evie . . . It's not impossible. But it might be better to think of it just as another dream. It is best for you to not get your dreams and memories confused. The past is the past. You are Evie. You are not Isabella. I am Leo. I am not Santiago. Let's forget about the Talent. Let's forget about the Amazon. This is the present. This is real. This life here. In Lofting. Let's just focus on that.'

He glugged down the last of his coffee.

And Evie got ready for another day at Lofting High.

Ramesh

On her way to her new school Evie passed a stern-looking man in a green wax jacket walking a springer spaniel. The springer spaniel – like all springer spaniels – was totally weird and very friendly. It began to sniff and pant and wag enthusiastically in Evie's direction.

'Hello. Hello. How are you? I am happy. Life is good. Like me. Like me. Do you like me?' were the thoughts speeding around the dog's brain. 'You smell of clean. Clean and coconut. I don't even know what a coconut is, but you smell of it.'

The dog's owner yanked back hard on the lead.

'Agh! I wish he knew how much that hurt.'

Evie looked at the man. A man with a long, hard solemn face. 'Excuse me, but—'

She was on the verge of telling him.

It took Evie every ounce of strength she had in her not to tell the man that the dog didn't like it. And she hated herself for not doing so. But she had promised her dad and Granny Flora, and she knew she had to keep a low profile. The Talent had to stay hidden.

So she just patted the dog's head and carried on walking to school.

Evie hadn't spoken properly with Leonora for a year now, ever since the argument about the Maltese terrier, even though they had both moved up to Lofting High School together. Leonora was the most popular girl in school, even among the older kids, who sometimes asked for her autograph, and she ignored Evie entirely, except for the odd whisper or giggle about her with her new gang of girls, who all looked like replicas of Leonora.

Evie, on the other hand, didn't have many friends at all.

She had become so scared about sharing secrets that she tended to shut up around people. The only person at school she liked talking to was called Ramesh, a boy with long, shiny black hair and a deep voice for an eleven-year-old. He was into guitar music and retro video games and scary animals. His mum was in charge of Lofting Zoo.

They were in a maths class together working

on something called Pythagoras' theorem. It was to do with triangles. The only bit Evie had liked was at the start, when Mrs Azikiwe had told them that Pythagoras was an Ancient Greek genius philosopher and maths whizz, who believed animals had souls and was a vegetarian before it was trendy.

But then the lesson grew boring.

Even Mrs Azikiwe seemed bored. 'So,' she said, sleepily, 'Pythagoras discovered that the square of the hypotenuse – the side opposite the right angle – is equal to the sum of the squares of the other sides. So, you can use it to calculate the length of any of the sides on a right-angled triangle or the distance between two points . . . On your worksheets, look at question six and see if you can discover the length of the side marked "a".' Then Mrs Azikiwe plonked herself on her chair and rubbed her forehead and gazed up at the ceiling.

'Hypotenuse is a good word,' Ramesh whispered, staring blankly at the worksheet. 'Hy-pot-e-nuse.'

'Sounds like a newspaper for hippos . . .' said Evie.

Ramesh smiled. 'I like that.'

A couple of minutes went by, as they tried to

work out the length of side 'a' on their worksheet.

Mrs Azikiwe was now asleep in her chair.

Ramesh had a sad look about him, Evie noted. He smiled a lot, but there was a sadness to him. She wanted to know what made him sad, but you can't just ask new friends about stuff like that. So she asked him about the zoo.

Evie thought in an ideal world *all* animals would be free. But she knew Lofting Zoo was one of the better ones. It looked after species that were nearly extinct.

'What's your favourite animal?' Evie asked him, in a whisper. 'In the zoo?'

'Well, I like the meerkats. They're cool. But I like saltwater crocodiles. And we don't have them. They're the most dangerous animal in the world.'

Evie shook her head. 'Nope. They're not.'

'Are you kidding?' said Ramesh, a little too loud. He lowered his voice. 'The saltwater crocodile can kill anything. On land or water. It can kill wild buffalo. Even sharks. It grabs them in its jaws and does a death roll.'

Evie sighed her disagreement. 'The saltwater crocodile is actually not even in the top three most dangerous animals.'

'Oh, so you're counting humans?'

Evie cleared her throat. 'Well, humans are the deadliest animal. No question. We kill each other. And we've wiped out millions of other animals. According to *National Geographic* the rate of species extinction happens one thousand times faster because of humans. Two hundred species of plants and animals go extinct every day. And if we're not careful we're going to wipe out the giant panda and the blue whale and the Asian elephant. They're all on the endangered list.'

'I know, it totally sucks.'

'But even if you don't count humans, the saltwater crocodile is not the deadliest animal.'

Ramesh doodled next to a picture of a triangle. 'What is, then?'

'Easy. Mosquito. They kill three million people a year. By spreading really, really dangerous dis—'

Just then Mrs Azikiwe woke up with a start and told them off for talking. So Evie and Ramesh went back to their geometry.

But in the afternoon break they kept the conversation going as they sat on a bench in the yard.

'You know a lot about animals,' Ramesh said.

Evie shrugged. She felt uncomfortable suddenly and started rambling.

'Not really,' she said. 'I mean, I know *facts*. I know that 10 per cent of a cat's bones are in its tail.

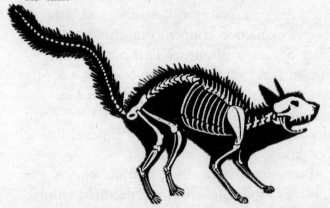

'I know that a hummingbird's wings beat up to seventy times a second. I know that chickens are the closest living relative to the Tyrannosaurus rex.

'I know a platypus swims with its eyes closed. And that the heart of a shrimp is located in its head.

'And that giraffes have black tongues to stop them getting sunburn, and – on the subject of giraffes – male giraffes sometimes drink the wee of female giraffes . . .'
Ramesh gagged. 'Wow. Gross.'

83

'But facts aren't really the only kind of knowledge,' Evie continued. 'I mean, imagine if you could actually know what it feels like, inside their heads . . . Inside the mind of a hippopotamus. Inside the mind of a goldfish. Inside the mind of a cat.'

Ramesh smiled. He liked this idea. 'That's what I always wonder. When I am at the zoo. Imagine what it'd be like to talk to a *giraffe* . . . Or any animal that wasn't us.'

'Yes,' sighed Evie. 'Imagine.'

'Mind you, I doubt animals would say very nice things to us. We're a cruel species.'

And just at that moment Leonora looked over at Evie and Ramesh and laughed with her new group of friends. Evie was pretty sure the laughter was aimed at her and Ramesh.

Evie put her head down. 'Yeah,' Evie agreed. 'A cruel species.'

Ramesh looked at Leonora and her gang giggling. 'Hey, on Saturdays I help out at the zoo. Do bits and bobs for my mum. Mainly, though, I just hang around. If you wanted to come along, I can give you a behind-the-scenes tour. We've got some cool creatures.'

Evie smiled. She thought of her dad, and of Mortimer J Mortimer. 'Thanks, but I can't.'

84

'Why?'

And Evie was thankful that the school bell went just at that moment, so she didn't have to answer the question.

The Power of Reptiles

When Evie got back from school, Granny Flora was there, sitting in the living room, chewing on liquorice. She held out the packet. 'Do you want one?'

Evie took a sweet. 'Thank you, Granny. What are you doing here?'

'I came to see you.'

'Where's Dad?' Evie asked, putting the liquorice in her mouth.

'He's out. He told me earlier he had to pick up a sofa from somewhere. I need to talk to you.'

Evie was confused. 'Why?'

Granny Flora looked worried. Evie had never seen Granny Flora look worried. And seeing Granny Flora look worried made Evie feel worried.

It was all very worrying.

'What's the matter, Granny Flora?'

'Plato,' she said.

'Is he hurt?'

'No, buttercup. It's worse than that.'

86

Evie's eyes widened.

'The thing you should know is that Plato is a bearded dragon and bearded dragons are lizards and lizards are reptiles. And reptiles are . . .' Granny Flora looked around, as if the right word was somewhere floating in the air. '. . . *Special*. Reptiles are special. They are different to other animals. They have powers. They know things. I think it's because reptiles have been around for a long time.'

Evie knew this, of course. Evie knew that reptiles had been around for more than 300 million years, from the murky swamps of the late Carboniferous period. But she didn't know what this had to do with Granny Flora sitting in the living room eating liquorice on a Tuesday evening.

'Plato speaks to me in riddles,' said Granny Flora. 'It's not always clear what he means. But on this he was very clear about one thing. I have made a mistake.'

'What was the mistake?' Evie asked, as she saw her dad — red-faced and exhausted — carrying a sofa outside the window.

'I have to teach you,' said Granny Flora as Evie's dad rested the sofa on the pavement to catch his breath. 'I have to help you develop the Talent. It's very important. Your life depends on it . . . But it has to be a *secret*. Not even your dad can know. It would put him in grave danger.' Evie's dad was now opening the front door. 'Do you understand?' whispered Granny Flora urgently.

Evie did not understand. Not at all. But she could see in Granny Flora's milky eyes that she was deadly serious.

'Yes, Granny,' she said. 'Of course.'

The Lesson

Every Sunday during that first term of high school, Evie went around to see Granny Flora for art class. That's what they told Evie's dad. And Granny Flora even prepared a work of art for Evie to take home. A picture of a cat that got a bit more complete every week.

'So,' said Evie on the first afternoon, staring at the bearded dragon as he ate from his chipped saucer of asparagus and mealworms in Granny Flora's garden, 'why are we trusting Plato on this?'

Plato tilted his head towards the sunshine.

Granny Flora giggled. 'Buttercup, I've told you. Plato knows everything. We have to trust him. He's never been wrong before.'

Evie studied the bearded dragon.

'But . . . we don't want to end up like mum.'

Granny Flora creaked forward in her wooden deckchair and reached for Evie's hand. 'I know, but Plato says we'd be in more danger if the Talent fades.'

89

As Granny Flora spoke Plato's spiky beard grew larger and turned brown to black. Evie tried to mind read him but couldn't. She felt that strange weakness she'd experienced around him before. 'Okay. Okay. Who are we going to start with, Plato himself?'

Granny Flora shook her head and chuckled as if she had never heard anything so ridiculous.

'You can't *start* with Plato. You **END** with Plato. You **START** with a liquorice.'

'You want me to mind-read a liquorice?'

'No, buttercup. I want you to taste one. Because I don't think you've ever tasted liquorice before.'

Now it was Evie's turn to laugh. 'You give me them all the time.'

'Yes. And I've seen you. You gobble it up. And then it's gone and you've hardly noticed it. Now, here is a liquorice. Pop that in your mouth and this time keep it there and really taste it. Let the world slip away so there is nothing at all but the sweet flavour.'

So Evie did just that. She let everything slip away. She concentrated on it and realised Granny Flora was right. She hadn't really tasted liquorice before. Hadn't noticed all the subtle types of sweetness in there. And even some

90

saltiness. And bitterness. It wasn't a totally wonderful taste but it wasn't a totally unpleasant one. Evie thought that if a taste could sum up life – the range of good and bad and in-between – then it would probably be liquorice.

'You see,' said Granny Flora, 'animal thoughts are like liquorice. You don't have to change a liquorice to taste it differently. And you don't have to change an animal. You don't have to get an animal to think. Animals are thinking all the time. And their thoughts talk to us all the time. It's just we haven't been paying attention.'

'I see,' said Evie. Though she wasn't sure she did.

'Different animals have different kinds of minds,' said Granny Flora. 'Whereas a dog thought can just arrive in your mind, simple and complete, like a slipper dropped on the carpet, a lizard thought is something that darts around, hard to catch.'

There was a cat sitting on Granny Flora's fence. The cat was a ginger tabby that Evie had seen before. It was the same one that had been hiding under the car from Scruff a year ago. Marmalade.

'Right,' said Granny Flora. 'You can start with that cat over there on the wall.'

Evie smiled. 'Well, that's easy.'

Granny Flora gave a low chuckle. 'I don't want you just to *understand* the cat. I want you to persuade it. I want you to get the cat to come over with nothing but your mind.'

Evie gulped. 'What? That's impossible. You can't tell a cat what to do. That's the whole point of cats. Cats don't obey. No Talent is that strong.'

'Believe me. There is someone with a Talent so strong that they could get a whole army of cats to do anything.'

For a moment Evie wondered if Granny Flora was talking about Mortimer J Mortimer, but she was too scared to find out. Mortimer J Mortimer was already scary enough in her mind.

So Evie tried it.

She stared deep at the cat as it licked a front paw.

'That's it,' said Granny Flora. 'Focus on the subject. Imagine there is nothing else in the world than that particular cat sitting on the wall.'

Evie let the world fade away. Until there was nothing but the ginger cat licking its right front paw with careful strokes of its tongue.

'Now,' said Granny Flora. 'Bow and arrow. Imagine your mind is a bow, and the thought is an arrow. Pull back, and speak a thought into the cat's mind.'

Evie did just that. 'Hello, Marmalade. I would like you to come over here, please.'

Marmalade stopped licking its paw and looked over at Evie. 'Now why would I want to do that?'

'Well,' said Evie, feeling how content the cat was, sitting on the wall, 'because it's nice here. And because I'm telling you.'

'That's not a reason. Sardines are a reason.'

Granny Flora pressed her hand on Evie's shoulders. 'No bribery. Remember. He has to come simply because you are mentally telling him to.'

Evie took a deep breath and tried again. 'Come here, Marmalade. Come here, Marmalade. Please come, Marmalade . . .'

Marmalade looked over at Evie and stood up, and for a moment – for a brief and wonderful moment – Evie thought that it had worked. She thought that she could do it, persuade a cat.

Then the cat jumped off the wall, but away from Evie, not towards her. Into the neighbour's garden.

'Oh no, he's gone,' said Evie.

93

Grandma Flora made a tutting sound. 'Oh, he's not gone. Watch this.'

And Evie watched Grandma Flora stare intently at the wall, as if trying to see something *beyond* that wall, then close her eyes. She looked deep in concentration.

A second later, the cat jumped back into view, onto the wall, then into the garden, trotting all the way over to Granny Flora.

Evie's jaw dropped open. 'How?' she said. '*How?*'

Marmalade stroked his head against Granny Flora's ankles, which looked like they were frowning because of her wrinkly tights. 'And not a single sardine in sight,' she chuckled. 'You see, your problem was that you were *asking* Marmalade to come to you. You need to make it INEVITABLE. You need not a shadow of doubt. You need to *become him*. Don't just understand the animal, *be* the animal.'

'Right. But—'

'You need to stop asking the cat to come down off the wall and *be* the cat coming down off the wall.'

Evie rubbed her face with both hands, as if washing her face with an invisible flannel. 'That sounds impossible.'

'Everything is impossible until you can do it. And you'll do it. It's a kind of seeing you don't need your eyes for. A kind of *tasting* but with your mind. Every animal is connected to every other animal. We are all linked. It's the chain of life. We all had a common ancestor four million years ago . . .'

Evie knew this. She also knew that there were more than six thousand groups of genes all animals had in common.

'Life is life,' said Granny Flora. 'Everything connects. Not just a grandma to a granddaughter. But a human to a chimpanzee, and primates to dogs and cats. Obviously we are related to some creatures more than others. We are actually closer to rabbits and rodents than cats and dogs, but the connections are all there. It's one big jigsaw of life. Every piece depends on every other piece. And it is all connected. It's all one big connecting energy. And humans don't have a word for it. But other animals do. It's called the *dawa*. It's like a river. It flows through everything. It connects all life on this earth together. Sparrows to dogs to snakes to fish. Even to trees.'

'Dawa,' Evie said, as if saying the word out loud could help her understand it.

'And to become a true Talent, you will have to be able to feel the dawa. You will have to truly understand that your life is not just contained in your body. It is a part of *every living thing*. It's an odd idea at first, but you'll get it.'

'Will I, Granny?' Evie said, staring at a daisy amid the grass.

'Oh yes, Evie. Oh yes. You'll get there. I know it. But you need to surround yourself with as many animals as possible. Every species. Exotic animals.'

'But you said bearded dragons are—'

'Difficult. Yes, they are. Absolutely. The most difficult of all. Which is why you need variety. To get to that level. To understand all the connections of life. Because you will need the Talent for more than cats and dogs. Anything could be coming your way . . .'

Evie thought. And then she thought some more.

And then she thought it was time to ask her dad a question.

And she would, when she got home, but first she was going to practise on any animal she could find in Granny Flora's garden. She tried it on a slug that Granny Flora spotted climbing a cracked flowerpot.

'Now, remember what I said. Focus on the creature with your eyes at first. But then close your eyes. And focus with your mind. With closed eyes, concentrate on the darkest part of the darkness. The part darker than liquorice, right in the centre. Then, ultimately, you will find the dawa.'

Evie stared at the slug. Then closed her eyes.

'The challenge with mind-talking to a slug, or to any gastropod, for that matter,' continued her grandmother, 'is in staying awake. They have the most boring minds in the universe. And if you'd ever met your grandfather, that's saying something.'

Evie laughed as she focused on the slug. But then the thoughts came – very slow and *sluggish* thoughts about soil – *soil!* – and Evie fell fast asleep instantly, dropping like a rubber tree in the Amazon as she collapsed on the lawn.

'See?' said Granny Flora, tapping Evie's cheek to wake her. 'Told you.'

The Boy Who Wanted to Talk to Horses

Walking home from Granny Flora's the day of the slug, Evie saw someone she hadn't seen in a while, sniffing around a bin. A large dog with matted fur and a wagging tail.

'Hello, Scruff,' Evie said.

Scruff didn't have to turn around. He could smell her.

'Oh. I'm good enough to talk to now, am I?'

Evie remembered that when she'd last seen Scruff she'd ignored him because she had been with her dad and she had still been trying to ignore animal thoughts in the hope they would go away. Now – since Granny Flora's warning – things were different, and she felt guilty.

'I'm sorry, Scruff, I really am . . .' she thought. Then she tried what she had tried on the cat. 'Come here, Scruff . . .' But that had no effect, so she pretended she *was* Scruff. She remembered what Granny Flora had said. *Don't just understand the animal, be the animal.* She closed her eyes and tried to find the dawa – the life that was in her, that was also in the dog. And she tried to implant a thought in Scruff's brain: 'I want to come to Evie.'

But it was no good.

'Your mind control won't work with me, Evie,' said Scruff.

'Sorry, I was just testing something.'

'And I was just sniffing something. Something delicious. Pizza in a pizza box. I like you, but I also like pizza. Life is good. Life is good . . .'

Evie left Scruff to his sniffing and walked a little further down Grafton Street.

A little boy with wild curly hair was playing in his front garden. He couldn't have been more than five years old. Six at the most. His mum was watching him from an inside window as he watered some flowers with a watering can that looked a bit too heavy for him.

He saw Evie and he looked at her strangely.

'It's you, isn't it?'

'What?'

'I saw you. With the dog. Scruff.'

Evie's eyes went wide. 'Scruff? How do you know his name?'

99

'He told me. He told me your name too, Evie.'

The boy kept watering the plants and Evie kept a fake friendly smile going because the boy's mother was still looking at her from behind the window.

'I can talk to dogs,' the curly-haired boy continued. 'But not cats. Only dogs. Please can you teach me? I want to talk to *all* animals . . .'

Evie was scared. Not *of* the boy, but *for* him. He had no idea about how dangerous it was to be open about such things. 'Who knows you have the Talent?' Evie asked.

The boy seemed confused, so Evie put it another way. 'Who knows that you can talk to animals?'

'No one. My mummy, but she thinks I'm being silly.'

'Good. Good. Don't tell anyone else, okay?' Evie waved at the mother behind the glass. She wanted to ask the boy a million questions. But she felt it best to get away from him. 'Right, I'd better go.'

'I want to talk to animals. Big animals. I want to talk to horses. Have you ever talked to a horse?'

Evie was already walking away. 'Bye.'

'Evie, my name's Sam.'

'Bye . . . Sam.'

'Bye, Evie.'

And Evie kept walking home, with a strange worry in her belly, as if the danger Granny Flora had warned her about had suddenly come a little closer.

The Jaguar

Later that week, Evie and her dad were taking bags of glass and cardboard along to be recycled.

'How are you getting on at school?' asked her dad, as they reached the bottle bank. 'Any new friends? Any nice people?'

'Well, there's a boy called Ramesh who seems okay. His mum works at the zoo.'

She watched her father grow pale. It was as if she had said a swear word. The *worst* swear word.

'He helps out sometimes, too.' Evie dropped an empty bottle in the bank and waited for it to smash. Then she dared to ask her dad the question. 'He's asked me to come over and see all the . . .' She paused, knowing her dad wouldn't like this idea. 'All the animals. And so I just wondered if I could go along . . . this Saturday.'

Her dad looked shocked, and frowned as he pulled an empty cereal box from the bag.

'I thought you didn't like the idea of zoos,'

he said eventually. 'I thought you didn't think animals should be in captivity, that all animals should exist as freely as nature intended.'

This was true, strictly speaking. But she had to practise the Talent with as many species as possible – Granny Flora had said so – and this seemed like a good opportunity.

'Dad, *please*.'

Her dad stared at the empty bottle of olive oil in his hand, like an actor holding a skull. And then he looked at his daughter.

'What about Leonora?'

'She doesn't speak to me any more. She hangs around with mean people. Ramesh is my only friend at the moment. Well, I don't even know if he's a proper friend. But he's good to talk to. He's the only one at school who likes talking about weird animal facts.'

And her dad just sighed and looked at her for a very long time, as if there was an important decision-making meeting going on in his head. 'Okay,' he said, after that long time. 'You can go to the zoo. But be very careful, do you understand?'

And Evie nodded and said that yes, she did understand, and felt excitement inside her. She had never been to a zoo before. And now she would finally hear the thoughts of animals she'd never heard before, at least not since she could remember. And, according to the zoo website, there were all kinds of exciting creatures there. Gazelles, hippopotamuses, elephants, orangutans, sea lions, actual lions, Sumatran tigers, lowland gorillas, meerkats and a Galapagos tortoise.

Her father emptied the last of the cardboard into the recycling bin. 'Just promise me you won't do anything out of the ordinary.'

'I promise.'

'And can I just ask you something, Evie?'

'Sure. Anything.'

'You haven't had that dream again, have you?'

'What dream?'

'The one about the snake and the frog?'

'Um, no,' said Evie.

This was a lie. And her dad looked at her doubtfully.

'Be careful, Evie. That's all I ask.'

That night, Evie had a different dream about the jungle.

In the dream, she was a little girl and her mum was there.

Her mum took her on a walk, telling her

about all the beautiful creatures they saw – glass frogs, toucans, scarlet macaws, and so on. She warned her about dangerous ones. Rattlesnakes. Red-bellied piranhas. Electric eels. Poison dart frogs. And she even told Evie about a Brazilian wandering spider.

Evie desperately tried to warn her. 'Mum, I have to tell you something about that spider. It will ki—'

'Sssh!'

Her mum had seen something.

Just as they were reaching the clearing where their hut was, it was there in front of them. A big cat – a beautiful and deadly jaguar, with golden fur and speckled black markings – prowling towards them.

'Get inside the hut, Evie.'

'Mummy?'

'Get. Inside. The. Hut.' Evie didn't. She just stood there, frozen with terror.

Her mum walked *towards* the jaguar and stroked it. Evie's mum closed her eyes and the jaguar walked away as if it had suddenly changed its mind about eating them.

Then there was a jump in time, inside the dream.

She saw her mother talking to a man. A tall

man in smart clothes with a bushy black moustache.

Mortimer J Mortimer.

Mortimer was standing with a lot of other men behind him. Loggers. They were standing in front of a white lorry with a chopped-down tree strapped to the back of it.

Evie noticed the man's right hand. She could see it more clearly than in the photograph. On the back of the hand and forearm there was a black tattoo of a coiled snake with its jaws open and its tongue out.

Her mum was upset. 'You are not going to destroy this part of the forest. There are endangered animals here. And tribespeople. The Huaorani people. This is their home. No way.'

And she said some words that Evie hadn't understood, but which sounded rude.

Then her dad appeared and told her mum to calm down and that was that. That was where the dream ended.

When she woke up she wanted to know if it had been a memory or not. So she went online and typed two words into a search box.

Huaorani people

There were 134,700 results.

Evie scanned her brain but she was sure she had never read about the Huaorani people, which could mean only one thing.

That wasn't just a dream. It was a *memory*.

Orwell the Elephant

Evie was excited.

It was the first thing they were going to do, this Saturday morning at Lofting Zoo. Feed the elephants.

Ramesh handed Evie a bucket full of bananas from a room called the Feeding Centre and then they walked a short distance, past two air-headed giraffes ('Hello, down there'), to the largest space in the whole zoo – the elephant enclosure.

Ramesh's mother was already there, handing bananas to one of the larger female elephants. Mrs Sengupta was a kindly twig-like woman with wild hair that refused to stay in her ponytail, wearing, like Ramesh was, the yellow sweater that was the Lofting Zoo uniform.

'Hello there!' she said with a kindly smile. 'You must be Evie. Come and say hello to Leonie!'

Leonie, the elephant Mrs Sengupta was feeding, took the green banana, wrapping it around the end of her curling trunk and bringing it to her mouth. 'Exquisite,' said Leonie. 'What a wonderfully yummy piece of fruit. I am blessed.'

Evie waved. 'Hello Mrs Sengupta! Hello Leonie!'

After a little while with Leonie, Mrs Sengupta suggested they go and feed an elephant in the corner of the enclosure, near a tree. This was Orwell, a male elephant. The tree he was next to had a pale trunk because the male elephants had stripped its bark with their tusks and then eaten it.

'All elephants like to eat,' said Ramesh. 'But Indian elephants *really* like to eat. I mean, that's all they do.' He held a banana in his hand for Orwell to take. 'Eat, eat, eat, poo, eat, eat, drink, eat, eat, sleep, eat. But mainly eat.'

Orwell was, apparently, Ramesh's favourite animal in the whole zoo. Evie felt a slight sense of calm sadness as Orwell's thoughts trod into her head.

'This makes things better,' said the elephant, swallowing the fruit whole. 'Bananas make everything better. They nearly make the sadness go away.'

'Why are you sad?' asked Evie, handing Orwell a new banana, and trying to look as

109

natural as possible so Ramesh didn't suspect anything, even as she had a mind-to-mind telepathic conversation.

'You . . . understand me?'

'Yes. I understand all animals. Well, most. Well, some. It's called the Talent. A few humans have it. I am trying to get better at it. It's quite important that I get better at it. That's what Granny Flora says. I am trying to feel the dawa . . . the thing that connects every living thing. Do you know the dawa?'

'Of course,' said Orwell. 'Every animal understands the dawa. It's what connects everything.'

Evie smiled. 'Anyway. I shouldn't have asked that question.'

'About the dawa?'

'No. About being sad.'

Orwell had eaten three more bananas by the time Evie had finished speaking.

'It's all right,' said the elephant. 'I'm sad because I've been thinking about when my mother died. Back when we lived in the Old Land. The hot place. Men with guns shot my mother. And I saw it with my own eyes. And it was terrible. I had nightmares. Did you know elephants have nightmares? I woke up wailing every morning. At the orphanage in the Old Land. And even when I first came here. I never got over it. But you know that pain, too, don't you?'

Ramesh tipped his bananas into Evie's near-empty bucket then went back to get some more. Evie was still shocked, staring in silence at Orwell's sad right eye. The only one she could see.

'My mother died too, yes,' Evie said with her mind. She even whispered it. 'How did you know?'

'Elephants always know. We understand the pain of others. Like yours. And the boy's. It's a terrible curse.'

'I'm sorry,' said Evie. 'About what happened to your mother. Humans can be a terrible

112

species. They sometimes don't care for other animals. They sometimes struggle to care for other humans.'

Orwell sighed in agreement, taking a brief pause between bananas. 'You seem like one of the good ones.'

Then Evie thought of something. 'You mentioned the boy. He had pain. Did you mean Ramesh? Is he in pain?'

The elephant took Evie's last banana. Ramesh, in the distance, headed towards them. 'Yes. Since his dad died. He normally cries with me. When no one else can see. I knew his dad. He was a good person, too. But then he got very ill and he couldn't see me any more. He died. But not like my mother. It was a long dying. And Ramesh was in a lot of pain. He still is. But he seems happy, now. That you are here. He needs a friend.'

And Ramesh was right there now, with a bucket overflowing with unripe green-yellow bananas. 'Here we go,' he said breezily.

Evie noticed a little boy waving at her, in the distance, from behind the fence. It was Sam, the boy with curly hair. The boy who was probably no more than six years old. Who she'd seen watering his front garden a few days

113

before. The one who wanted her to teach him how to talk to animals.

Evie waved back.

'Who's that?' Ramesh asked.

'No one. I don't know. Just a friendly kid.'

And Evie tried to hide her relief as Sam was dragged away to see some other animals.

The Reptile House

Evie listened to as many animals as possible as they walked around the zoo. She heard a sea lion moaning about visitors. 'For pity's sake, they think I'm a seal. I am **NOT** a seal. It's so insulting.'

'I know you're not a seal,' said Evie. 'I can see you have your ears on the outside and that you are walking on your flippers, not bouncing on your belly.'

The sea lion understood and waved at her. 'Thank you. It's nice to be understood. Be your own self, that's what my mum said. Never be a seal.'

'That's good advice,' Evie thought-spoke. 'Well, the first bit.'

In the aquarium she met a happy male seahorse who was pregnant, swimming along with his partner, their tails hooked around each other.

'Oh Lana,' he said. 'I'm just *so* happy.'

'Yes, Bob, me too. And you are positively **BLOOMING**.'

They then went to see the Sumatran tigers.

115

One of the tigers stared right at Evie, as he paced his side of the perimeter fence. 'And what are YOU looking at?' he asked her.

'Nothing,' thought Evie, backing away. 'Just admiring your beauty.'

'Well, thanks. That's kind of you. Are you related to a woman called Flora, by any chance?' the tiger asked. 'She had the Talent, too.'

'Yes!' said Evie. 'She's my granny.'

'Well I never! Please tell her my grandfather says hi.'

'I certainly will,' smiled Evie, as Ramesh pointed for them to turn left. Left towards the fruit bats.

They walked into a darkened cave. Evie thought the fruit bats looked cute, with their furry fox-like faces. Bat thoughts crowded her and flapped in her mind.

'Hey!'

'Over here!'

'I come close but I never touch!'

'Whoo!'

'Zoooooom!'

'This isn't flying! This is AIR BALLET!'

'I love watermelon!'

Evie chuckled and Ramesh looked at her quizzically. 'What?' he said.

'Nothing,' she replied. 'I just love animals.'

He smiled at her. 'I can tell.'

Ramesh ushered Evie to the reptile house. The reptile house was what Evie was most excited about. It was also the place, she was sure, where she would be able to strengthen her Talent.

The reptile house was a large, low building in the centre of the zoo.

The first creature she saw wasn't technically a reptile. It was an amphibian with a flat body, a wide flat head, tiny blue eyes and a large mouth. It walked slowly around underwater ignoring Evie and Ramesh completely.

'Ah, cool,' said Evie. 'An axolotl. I love them.'

'You know about axolotls?'

Evie felt insulted he would even ask such a thing. 'I know they used to be considered monsters . . . which is totally unfair. Because they don't go around being very scary. In fact, they're the ones who get picked on all the time. Fish come up to them and bite bits off them. Their little fingers. But they grow back. They don't let the bullies get them down.'

Ramesh nodded, impressed. 'Wow. You really know your monsters. Did you also know that they are nearly extinct in the wild? Because of pollution. And that's why this zoo is one of the better ones . . . I know you're, like, totally against animals being kept captive.'

'Uh huh,' said Evie. 'It seems a bit unfair. It's like a prison but the only crime they've committed is not be a human.'

'Yeah, I get the principle, Evie. It's just that humans have messed up the world so much some animals can't even exist in the wild. But this zoo has more protected species than most. It takes animals that are in danger in the wild. To keep them alive and to . . .'

Ramesh kept talking but Evie stopped listening. She was trying to focus and send her thoughts into the mind of the axolotl. She closed her eyes. She imagined a thought being an arrow, as Granny Flora had told her, and she tried to fire it into the reptile's head.

'Hello,' said the thought. 'Can you hear me? I am here. The tall human outside your tank.'

There was no response.

Evie tried again, and again, to communicate with the amphibian, but it was the same. There was nothing at all.

'Are you okay?' Ramesh asked.

'What do you mean?'

'You're just standing there, like you're in a trance . . . I've been talking to you for three minutes and you haven't heard a thing I've been—'

'Sorry. I just sometimes get these weird headachy things. It's fine now.'

They moved along. They saw an African bullfrog, a Caiman lizard, and then snakes – a king cobra, a puff adder, and the scariest-looking one of all. A giant, strong and sinister snake swimming around in a tank of water.

The green anaconda.

Evie read the sign next to the tank:

The anaconda is a semi-aquatic snake found in areas of tropical South America. The name refers to various snakes in the genus *Eunectes*, but it is commonly used to refer to one species – the green anaconda. Considering both length and weight, the green anaconda is the **largest snake in the world**, growing up to **9m long** and **weighing as much as 250kg.**

'I suppose you know all about anacondas too,' Ramesh muttered.

'A little,' Evie said, with a shrug.

'So how venomous are they?' Ramesh asked, with a smirk.

119

'Trick question. They're not venomous. They're constrictors. They wrap their bodies around their prey and squeeze until . . .'

Ramesh threw his arms around Evie and squeezed really hard. He clearly thought this was hilarious.

'Not funny,' said Evie, elbowing Ramesh in the stomach. Ramesh bent double and coughed from the blow.

Evie laughed hard. 'Oops! Sorry.'

But she stopped laughing because she felt a sudden coldness inside her brain. The anaconda was staring straight at her.

'*Trouble comes.*'

'What?' Evie asked, aloud. Then, with her mind, 'What trouble? I don't understand. What sort of trouble?'

'*Every kind.*'

'What do you mean?'

'*In your future. You are in mortal danger. And so is someone you love. It is coming, it is coming, it is coming . . .*'

And then the snake's giant head disappeared below the water again. And the coldness in Evie's brain was now accompanied by a tightness in her body. As if she wasn't just reading the anaconda's thoughts but getting crushed by them.

120

'Are you okay?' Ramesh asked, suddenly worried. 'You look terrified.'

'I can't . . . I can't breathe . . .' She felt a sudden need to step away, and so she started walking, then running, out of the reptile house. Out into air and sunlight, with Ramesh jogging behind.

'What's up?' he asked.

'I just felt a bit dizzy,' Evie lied. 'It's fine.'

Five minutes later Evie and Ramesh were at the chimpanzee enclosure.

They saw some teenagers, not from their school, who were all laughing at another boy who was standing in front of the chimpanzees, trying to do an impression of them.

'Oooh ack acka ooh ack ack acka,' said the boy, smiling at how funny he was.

But Evie wasn't really listening to the boy.

'It's so embarrassing,' said the chimpanzee closest to her. 'To think we are related to these hairless monkeys.'

'Oh Cynthia, don't,' said another, a male chimp, hanging upside down from a thick branch. 'You are SUCH a downer.'

But then they heard something.

'What was that?' said the first chimpanzee, Cynthia.

And Ramesh was asking the same question, out loud.

Evie heard it too now.

Screaming coming from beyond the aviary behind them.

Now it was Ramesh's face that was filled with panic. 'Oh no.'

'What?'

'The noise. The screaming. I know where it's coming from. It's the lion enclosure . . .'

They both started running, back through the reptile house and the aviary, until they were there, pushing their way through the crowds that were gathering. Some of these people were gasping or crying or wailing.

A woman spotted that Ramesh was wearing the yellow sweater that was the uniform of workers in Lofting Zoo. Even though Ramesh was twelve, he was tall and looked a bit older.

'Do something!' the woman cried. Evie felt she recognised her.

'What happened?' Ramesh asked.

'It's my son! He's fallen! He climbed up the fence! I tried to stop him! And . . . and . . . he's in there. He's in there with the lions. LOOK!'

The Lion's Den

Evie pushed through the crowd quickly, ahead of Ramesh.

Once at the fence, it took a few seconds for her to spot the boy.

She stared over the sunken enclosure at the lions.

And then she saw him.

A child. A little boy.

Evie turned back to Ramesh, who was a bit further back in the crowd.

'Do something!' Evie shouted. 'There's definitely a kid in the enclosure!'

She saw Ramesh looking in horror as he grabbed the walkie talkie from his belt. 'Calling all units! Emergency! There is a child in the lion enclosure! Repeat! **THERE IS A CHILD IN THE LION ENCLOSURE!** Mum! Everybody! **THERE IS A HUMAN CHILD IN THE LION ENCLOSURE!**'

Evie couldn't see clearly, the boy's back was turned, and he was standing near one of the trees. He had hurt himself and was hobbling

123

a little in pain. He walked forward, as the crowd gasped 'No!'

He was heading towards the four lions. Three were lying down but one – a strong and powerful-looking lion – was walking over towards the boy. A female, Evie realised, because it had no mane. Evie knew that it was the lionesses that were often the most dangerous. They were the ones who killed their prey for the rest of the pride to enjoy. But another lion, a male with a big bushy mane, was also standing up to see what was going on.

The walking lioness got close, then stopped and inspected the boy.

That was when Evie realised it was HIM.

The little boy in the red T-shirt with wild curly hair.

'Oh no,' said Evie.

It was *Sam*.

His mother, standing at the edge of the lion enclosure, screamed, 'Like a statue! Stand still like a statue!'

Meanwhile, the lioness skulked closer to little Sam. And began looking intently into his eyes.

Evie tried to blot out the noise of the crowd. She remembered what Granny Flora had taught her about liquorice. To concentrate on nothing else. She stared at the lioness's face, quite far away, and tried to let the world disappear.

She felt the lioness's mind prowl into her own.

'I need to eat the boy,' the lioness was thinking.

'He does look very tasty,' agreed the lion standing further behind.

Evie pictured a bow in her mind. And turned a thought into an arrow. Hard and sharp and to the point.

'No,' was the thought. 'No, don't eat the boy. He has a mother. He has people who love him. Please, don't eat the boy. Don't eat Sam.'

She was bright red with the effort of trying to make the lioness understand.

But she was too far away. There were too many people. There was too much commotion. The lioness took another step towards Sam.

'Make sure you share him with us,' said the male.

Evie looked around. She couldn't see Ramesh now. He was lost in the crowd. No one was looking at anything apart from the boy.

Someone who worked at the zoo was running over.

But there was still no one from the zoo inside the lion enclosure.

125

Evie looked at Sam. He was still hurt, but he had gone quiet.

She knew, suddenly, what Sam was doing in there.

He was trying to use the Talent on the lioness. He wanted to talk to her.

Evie remembered he had told her he couldn't talk to normal cats, so a lion was going to be impossible. And she knew that in a matter of seconds the lioness was going to do something.

Without another thought, Evie was climbing over the timber and metal fence.

'What the hell are you doing?' asked a man next to her, trying to grab her leg. She kicked his hand away.

'Sorry!' she said.

She was on the other side of the fence now, standing high on the outer rim, a ledge between the fence and the lower level of the enclosure floor.

There was a long drop to reach the lion area.

Evie fell onto the dry, yellowing grass and hurt her ankle.

Behind her she could hear Ramesh. 'Evie! Evie! Oh man. What are you doing?'

But Evie couldn't listen to the voices of

humans now. She had to focus on the lioness
– the lioness standing right in front of little Sam.

'I am going to eat the boy,' thought the
lioness, licking her lips. 'He looks a bit crunchy.
But tasty.'

Evie thought as hard and sharply as she could
and aimed the thought right between the
lioness's hungry eyes.

'*No.*'

The lioness saw her and flicked her tail.

'Yes,' said the lioness. 'Yes, I am going to eat
him. And then, after that, I am going to eat
you.'

'But you'll still share, right?' said the male
in the background. 'I'm getting **REALLY**
hungry.'

Evie continued staring at the lioness as Sam
turned around and saw her.

'It's you!' he said. 'I was waiting for you to
come . . .'

'What?'

'I knew it was safe if you were here!'

She put her finger to her lips, but there was
no shushing him.

'Tell me how to speak to the lion! I want
to speak to a lion! Please!'

Evie could see he had a rip in his jeans

127

where he had fallen. And his knee and hands were bleeding a bit.

She needed to get closer to him. She needed to get between Sam and the lioness.

The Queen of Beasts

Above her, and all around, the crowds of zoo visitors were still lost in horror. Well, apart from the people who were filming it all on their phones.

'We don't want to hurt you,' Evie told the lioness. 'Come on. We have people who love us. Please . . .'

'Why should I care about you humans? You don't care about me. You just come to point and take photos.'

Evie had a quick glance around for some sign of help, but there was nothing. Ramesh was nowhere to be seen.

She was scared, suddenly. Lions were hard creatures to argue with. And also, if you lose an argument with a lion you end up as lunch, which is not a great way to end up.

The lioness walked closer to Evie, ignoring the boy now.

The lioness growled at Evie. It looked ready to pounce.

She tried a different tactic.

'You're right,' thought Evie, staring hard into the predator's amber eyes. 'They don't care about you. Not really. Not next to a human life. So be careful what you do.'

Evie kept her eyes on the lioness, trying to make her face match the mind message.

The lioness didn't seem to be listening.

And then, a voice, shouting from the crowd. *'EVIE! STAND BACK!'*

It was Mrs Sengupta.

She was holding a kind of rifle. She was ready to fire at the lioness. Evie was pretty sure she would fire a tranquiliser dart rather than shoot the lioness. But Evie was also pretty sure the lioness wouldn't know that.

'Look! Look up there. If you so much as scratch either one of us, they will kill you. You will be dead. I'm sorry. But it's true. They will kill you. If you touch either the boy or me, they will kill you.'

The lioness looked up at the watching crowd, then back at Evie. Her thoughts came strong, like punches. 'You are lying. You are a bad liar. Your mind is as weak as a gazelle's.'

'No. It will happen. Please . . . if you hurt me, or the little boy, they will kill you.'

The lioness lifted her chin up and gave Evie

132

an arrogant glare. 'I am the queen of beasts. No one is in control of me.'

'Oh, really? Look around. Can you leave here if you want to? No. The humans are in charge here.'

The lioness looked to the side, then scratched her ear. For a moment she looked as innocent as a housecat. 'If I back down, I'll look weak.'

Evie thought, 'And if you don't back down, you'll look dead. Because, well, you'll be dead. Dead. Totally dead.'

Evie might have been overdoing it with the dead stuff, but it was getting through. It's the one thing all animals have in common: they don't like the idea of dying very much.

The lioness was thinking hard, as the three other lions came closer.

Evie tried to remember what Granny Flora had told her. She closed her eyes. She looked for the darkest part of her vision. The part like liquorice. But it was a sunny day, and the darkness of her closed eyes was more like a redness. But still she tried. She tried to find the dawa. The river of life that connected her to the lioness.

She remembered the words of Granny Flora. *Don't just understand the animal. Be the animal.*

There, in the sun-red blankness of her closed

133

eyes, she felt a strange stillness. She finally could sense she was getting close to it. The dawa! She focused on that darkness as it grew, imagining the lioness all the time – her face, her skulking movements, the voice of her thoughts . . . And then, suddenly, she felt like she wasn't there at all.

She saw herself from the lioness's perspective. Standing still, eyes closed. She saw Sam, too, who was starting to look scared, chewing his own fingers.

But in that same moment she also felt the force of the dawa. Granny Flora had told her that the first time she experienced it, it would be powerful. It entered her mind like a gale-force wind.

The lioness knocked her off her feet without even touching her. And as she landed on the grassy ground the connection was lost.

'What happened, Evie?' shouted Sam. 'Was that the lion in your mind? That is *so* cool.'

Evie, on the floor, saw a door slowly open in the enclosure. A zoo worker was there in the shadows. Ramesh! They had to escape to the door, but Evie knew an adult lion could run over fifty miles an hour pursuing its prey. So they couldn't run together without one of them being eaten. She decided to stay and distract the lioness.

'Sam,' she said quietly. 'When I stand up, you walk very slowly towards that open door, do you understand?'

But something had happened between the lioness and Evie. Something in that moment of touching the dawa.

'You're right,' the lioness said.

She turned to the other lions.

'The human girl is right,' she told them. 'It's not worth it.'

The male lion was disappointed. 'Well, your call, Delia. But wow, that would have been fun.'

Evie slowly stood up.

'Thank you. Thank you. Thank you.'

She walked over to Sam and took his hand. 'Come with me, and you'll stay alive,' she told him.

Sam stared at all four of the lions. Including the male one, still licking his lips. He could see the lion's sharp, hooked teeth.

He gulped. The little boy seemed to realise how foolish he had been.

And so they – Evie and Sam – walked calmly, steadily, watched by hundreds of faces and cameras, towards the open door, where Ramesh was standing, waiting for them.

What Evie's Dad Said

Evie's dad was in the garage fixing a broken wardrobe.

He was being very aggressive with a hammer and a nail, which resulted in him banging his own thumb. And this made him swear. But he wasn't just angry about the hammer. He was angry with Evie, and she knew it.

'Dad, I'm really, really sorry. But what else could I do?'

He ignored this question as he walked around holding his thumb.

'Are you *crazy*?'

Evie shrugged. 'No, Dad.'

'What were you *thinking*?'

Evie decided to be honest. 'I was thinking that no one else would have been able to communicate with the lioness. I was thinking that there was a good chance that I could save that boy's life. I was thinking I had no choice.'

'There is always a choice, Evie. And besides . . . even with the Talent, you can't just jump into a lion enclosure. Especially as you haven't used it in a long time.'

'I have used it,' she said.

'What? Evie! Why? After everything I told you.'

'I'm sorry, but ...' She stopped short of telling him that Granny Flora had been training her.

'You're lucky you weren't killed!'

'But I wasn't!'

'*Yet.*'

Evie was flummoxed. 'Yet? Yet? What do you mean?'

He walked over to a battered table full of crumpled papers and tools. He picked up his phone.

'Look. It's all over social media!'

Evie stared in horror as he showed her posts of the camera phone footage on YouTube and Facebook and Twitter and Instagram. Of her and Sam and the lion.

'Girl tames lion' was the title of the video.

She saw a news headline. '**GIRL SAVES BOY FROM LION'S DEN**'. And another: '**THE LION WHISPERER**'.

Just at that moment the doorbell rang.

Evie followed her dad through the garage and into the house and watched as he opened the door. Outside there was a smartly dressed woman holding a microphone, with a cameraman standing behind her.

'Hello Mr Trench, this is Scarlett Adams from BBC News. I just wondered if we could speak to your amazing daughter about what happened at the zoo today . . .'

'No. No, you can't.'

Scarlett Adams kept smiling. 'Well, maybe we could have a word with you, then? We have already spoken with the mother of the little boy – Sam – and apparently he believes he can talk to animals. With his mind.'

'What **NONSENSE!**' Evie's dad said.

'The boy said that Evie can do it, too. That's why the lion retreated. That's what he says. Does your daughter believe she can talk to lions, Mr Trench?'

'Of course she doesn't. Now, good day!'

As the door slammed in the news reporter's face, Evie's dad glared at her. He looked frightened more than angry. And then he quietly swore in Spanish. 'See! See what you've done. This is a nightmare.'

His phone started to ring.

'Hello?' he said. 'No . . . No, I do not want to talk to the *New York Times*. And nor does my daughter.' Then, when he had hung up the phone, Evie's dad said, 'It's international now. The *New York Times*! And now that blooming boy is telling the world you have the Talent. This is a nightmare! And you know why it is a nightmare, don't you?'

Evie nodded grimly. 'Mortimer.'

'Exactly.'

There Is No Normal

The next day was Sunday. Evie and Granny Flora were convincing her dad not to move. He had been halfway through packing everything in Evie's bedroom into cases.

'We can't stay here! He'll come for us . . .'

'Dad, we can't just run away. He'll come for the boy, too. That's all over the news as well. We can't just leave him here.'

'*Lo siento*. I'm sorry. That boy is not my responsibility, Evie; you are. My final promise to your mother, before the venom took over completely, was that I'd look after you. She just wanted me to keep you safe, Evie. We've got to go. And we'll take Granny Flora too.'

Up until this point, Granny Flora had been sitting in silence in the corner of the room, with Plato the bearded dragon on her knee. She had her eyes closed, as if in a deep trance. But now Granny Flora's eyes sprang wide open.

'NO!' she shouted.

Evie's dad was confused. 'No, what?'

140

'We can't move. We have to stay here. That's what Plato believes. If we leave, the trouble will end us. If we stay, we can end it.'

Evie's dad didn't like the sound of this. 'We can end it? We can end it? *¿Qué significa eso?* What does that mean?'

'I don't know,' said Granny Flora. 'I just know we have to stay. And wait.'

'And in the meantime?' wondered Evie, staring at the bearded dragon's mysterious ancient face.

Granny Flora popped a liquorice in her mouth. 'In the meantime, we carry on as normal.'

So that was what they did.

They carried on as normal. Or they tried to.

The trouble was, *nothing* seemed normal any more. Evie was gossiped about continually at school. She was now known as 'Lion Girl'.

She hoped the gossip would fade, but the whole day went by and she was still being laughed at. She tried to focus on other things. In her science class, she got an A for a biology test, possibly for knowing that when some plants are being eaten by caterpillars they send

141

chemical signals to wasps, who then come along and attack the caterpillars. In art, she drew a really detailed picture of Scruff, from memory. And ignored it when someone behind her whispered, 'She probably thinks she can talk to dogs, too.'

But it was the next day that things got really weird.

She was walking to school, thinking about the double history lesson she was about to have on the Ancient Romans, and whether she'd done her homework right, when she noticed an air of weirdness. And it wasn't just the usual kids from Lofting High shouting, 'Hey, Lion Girl!'

She passed Scruff, who was sniffing the air wildly. 'There is an air of weirdness,' he confirmed, as he trotted by.

Then she saw a cat in a window of one of the houses. The window was slightly open. Evie recognised the cat.

The ginger tabby.

Marmalade.

'*Help me,*' the cat was pleading, with its mind and miaow.

Evie turned away from the cat. After the lion incident she had newly promised her dad not to respond to any animals, and this time she knew she really had to keep that promise. She had to keep a low profile. So she carried on walking.

'Only you can stop this,' the cat went on. 'You have to stop this, before it's too late.'

Hearing this, Evie turned and walked back towards the house.

When she got there, something incredibly weird happened.

Marmalade squeezed out of the gap in the front window and leapt onto the grass.

'Marmalade? Marmalade?'

But he ran straight past Evie and down a side alley at full speed.

'Weird,' said Evie. 'Very weird.'

The Missing Posters

Closer to school, she saw something else weird.

A '**MISSING CAT**' poster stuck to a lamp-post. There was a photo of a cat. A posh-looking Persian cat.

She quickly scanned the words below the photo.

MISSING

My beloved cat LADY GAGA is missing from Sycamore Avenue. She has been missing since last night.

This is very strange because she has never left the house in her life before. Ever. In fact, she only ever leaves her basket if she needs the loo, or to eat her favourite Posh Paws cat food.

If you have any information please email MrsBloom@fastmail.com or text 072719735911.

REWARD £300.

This was weird.

But it got weirder.

There were more posters. But they weren't all posters of cats. Not completely. There *was* a poster of another cat – a chocolate-coated Burmese named Cocoa.

MISSING

Cocoa Our Burmese Cat

Cocoa hasn't been seen for two days. Although she likes to be outside, she normally walks on top of fences nearby. Please let us know if you see her. She responds to her name and the words 'cheddar time' (she likes cheese).

0128 69594

But then on the next lamp-post there was a poster of a missing Labradoodle called Mrs Cuddles.

MISSING

Mrs Cuddles

Our dog Mrs Cuddles has vanished. We left her in the house on Monday, and when we came back she was gone. She is a Labradoodle and a rescue dog and gets quite nervous when she is out of the house so we are worried. Please email sophie@loftingbakery.co.uk or text/call

07657219546.

Then one of a missing Shih Tzu.

MISSING

Cassandra

My poor dog, Cassandra, has vanished. She ran
straight out of the front door this morning and I
couldn't catch up with her. Most unusual. If you see
her, please contact me on Facebook. My name is
Cheryl Sanders. Or you can contact my husband, Pav.
Actually don't. He's useless.

And a French bulldog.

MISSING

Francis

Our little French disappeared while we were
at the park. I was chatting to a friend and
the next thing I knew he wasn't there. Which
was odd because I'd just thrown him a stick.
Please call

07274447906.

And a Yorkshire terrier.

MISSING

Stephen

If anyone has seen our Yorkshire terrier
please let us know. He's called Stephen.
He's very yappy. But he won't hurt you.
Unless you are a cat. In which case, he'll
probably try. Please contact me at
marcus@acutabovehairsalon.co.uk

And a Rottweiler.

MISSING

Our dog Charlotte

Please help us find our lovely dog Charlotte.
She disappeared from my car while I was
parked at the post office. Please call the
number below with info.

07287685944

And a dog with no breed.

MISSING

Falstaff

Our dog Falstaff is missing. He is a wild-looking thing with short legs and long pointy ears. If you see him, say the word 'biscuit' and he will come straight to you. Please contact me on

07499331627.

And a hamster called Cheryl.

MISSING

Cheryl

Cheryl is our daughter's pet hamster. Our daughter
is five years old and she has been crying for fifteen
hours. Please help us find her. Our daughter will
give you all her pocket money (£4.38). Call

067439788123

if you have any info.

153

And a tortoise called Flash.

MISSING

Flash

Our tortoise has gone missing from his
home in our garden. He hasn't left our
garden since 1992, when we took him to
the pub. We are very worried.
A reward of £100 is offered.
Please call us on

062544723100.

And a leopard gecko called Gordon.

MISSING

Gordon

Our leopard gecko is missing. He has been taken.
Please follow our Twitter page @searchforGordon
and contact us if you happen to see a
lost-looking leopard gecko.

#searchforGordon
#prayforGordon
#comebackGordon

Three unnamed ferrets.

MISSING

Help! I've lost my ferrets!
Contact Brian.
(I live above the chip shop.)

And a parakeet called Pablo.

MISSING

Our parakeet Pablo is missing. He lives in our attic but
this morning he wasn't there. The window was
smashed. He must have flown through it.
We are very confused.
Please email Laurence and Paul at
laurenceandpaul@theartshop.com

This is getting weirder and weirder, thought Evie. Cats went missing all the time. Even dogs did *sometimes*. But hamsters? Tortoises? Geckos? Parakeets? *All on the same day*?

But things were about to get even weirder than this.

She saw Leonora far ahead of her, typing on her phone, carrying a hockey stick.

As Evie passed Leonora's house she saw a tiny white fluffy dog sitting in the window. On guard. A little Maltese terrier with a pink ribbon in its long, perfectly groomed hair. It was Bibi. The dog who had been the reason for Leonora and Evie's falling out over a year ago.

The terrier yapped at the sight of her.

Most small dogs are yappy. Their yaps are also thoughts. Because for terriers there is very little difference between yapping and thinking.

'He's coming!'

That's all the yap said.

Over and over and over.

'He's coming! He's coming! He's coming! He's coming! He's coming!'

Evie tried to send a thought across the air and through the window and into the dog's brain. 'Who?' she asked.

And the Maltese terrier stopped yapping for a second and stared at Evie and cocked her head to the side and for a moment Evie thought she might get an answer. But no.

'He's coming!' came the yap again. 'He's coming!'

'**WHO IS COMING?**' Evie closed her eyes and tried to reach the dawa, that life-force that connected everything, even schoolchildren and Maltese terriers. But for some reason Bibi's mind seemed impenetrable. Harder even to step inside than the mind of a lion. All she could do was mind-talk. So she dared to ask another question. 'Is it a man called Mortimer?'

But she got no different answer. 'He's coming! He's coming!'

Maybe the dog's talking about Leonora's dad, Evie thought, as she moved away. *Maybe that is who is coming.*

And that was the thought she tried to keep in her head as she walked ahead to school and the abnormal day that awaited her.

The Weirdos

Evie sat with Ramesh on a bench in the schoolyard.

She was now, officially, the joke of the school.

She knew this because Jacob Jeffreys, who had been the joke of the school ever since he had peed the bed on a school trip to the Lake District, had come up to her and said, 'Thank you. I am no longer the joke of the school.'

'Great,' said Evie.

'Even with this spot on my nose,' said Jacob. It did look a particularly massive spot.

'Oh, yay,' said Evie sarcastically, 'happy to help.'

Jacob walked away.

'You can hang around with us, Jacob,' Ramesh called after him. 'We could all be jokes together. Like, a human joke society.'

Jacob carried on walking. Holding onto a book called *Aliens Are Real And May Be Among Us*. 'No, thanks. I'm not that desperate.'

Evie stared at Ramesh. 'You're not a joke.'

Ramesh laughed. 'Are you kidding me? At

my last school I used to get picked on for *everything.*'

Then he gave a list of *Everything He Used To Get Picked On About.* It included:

1. Having long hair.
2. Liking loud rock music from the olden days that his dad liked.
3. Being a vegan and a Hindu who was home-schooled until he was eight.
4. Being dyslexic.
5. Crying in assembly.

'Well,' said Evie. 'You're not a joke now.'

'Really?' he said cheekily. 'Even though I hang around with Lion Girl?'

Evie smirked. 'Well, okay. You are a bit of a joke. Yeah. Mainly, though, you are just annoying.'

Evie noticed Leonora and her gang of friends were looking over, so she tried to keep talking.

'How's your mum?' Evie asked Ramesh. 'I heard they're closing down the zoo for a little while . . .'

Ramesh nodded. 'A month. Mum's fine, though. She's just pleased no one got hurt.'

'I'm sorry,' said Evie.

'Hey, it's not your fault. You were just trying to help the little idiot. I mean, BOY. Even if you hadn't gone over it'd still be closed down. We might even be in a worse situation . . .' He looked up to the sky. 'Everyone really **DOES** think you can talk to animals, y'know? That's what the boy said you told him. Sam. It's all over the internet.'

Evie pulled at her hair and inspected it. 'I never told him that.'

'Oh.'

She stared at Ramesh. 'But it is true.'

'Whaaaaaaat? Don't mess with me.'

She took a deep breath. It was time. And Ramesh, her fellow joke, was the person to tell it to.

'I have something called the Talent,' she said matter-of-factly. 'It means I can communicate telepathically with animals. It is a skill that, once out in the open, puts me in great danger.'

Ramesh laughed and shook his head.

'I'm not joking,' Evie told him. 'I am incredibly serious.'

Ramesh could see she was serious, but still found it hard to believe. The wind blew his hair in front of his face and he pulled it behind his ears. He tried not to laugh.

162

'Prove it,' he said. 'Prove you are not just . . .'

'A weirdo?'

'Well, **I KNOW** you're a weirdo. But I'm a weirdo too. Weirdos are the way to be. Especially in a school full of NAUSEATING NORMALS. I mean, prove you're a WEIRDO WITH SKILLS.'

Beak to the Rescue

Evie tried to think how she could prove to Ramesh that she had the Talent.

'The lioness backed down. That's because I told her she could get killed.'

Ramesh shrugged. 'That's not proof. The lioness might not have been in the killing mood.'

'Oh, she was!'

'Right. Sure. You know that.'

'You saw me in the reptile house,' Evie urged. 'You thought I was acting a bit odd. That's because I was trying to communicate with the axolotl.'

'Ah,' said Ramesh, though Evie could see he was starting to wonder. 'Trying to and **ACTUALLY DOING SO** are very different things.'

'And the elephant – Orwell – he told me . . .'

Ramesh suddenly looked worried. 'What? What did the elephant tell you?'

She couldn't bring herself to say 'About your dad dying'. So she just said, 'Nothing.'

164

Ramesh looked out at the schoolyard and saw Leonora and the other girls pointing over.

'I miss him, you know,' he said, as if he understood what Evie had been going to say. 'Every day, I wake up and there's a moment I still think Dad's here. And then I realise that he's gone. That he'll never be able to go to the cinema with me, or tell me off about my messy room, and I find it too much . . .'

Evie nodded.

'You're a hero, mate,' Ramesh told her, being serious for a second. 'You probably saved that boy's life.'

They heard someone giggling and looked up to see Leonora getting closer, taking a picture of Evie with her phone.

'What are you doing?' Evie asked, worried her face was already too much on the internet.

Leonora smiled broadly. 'I'm taking a picture of you both. It's for a photography project for art class . . .' Her friends were laughing. Evie knew this was a lie.

'You generally ask someone before you take their picture,' mumbled Evie.

'Ooh, the lion roars!' said Leonora's friend, Anoushka. Anoushka was the girl you wanted

165

to be if you didn't like being the girl you were. And she was quite evil.

'I might put it on Instagram, too. Got 400,000 followers now. I just need a title for it. The picture, I mean. "Sad Boy and Lion Girl" . . . That might work.' She scratched her chin, as if thinking really hard. 'Or "The Girl Who Thought She Was Special Finds a Friend" . . . or just "Weirdos". Yeah, I like that. What you reckon, Livs?'

Leonora's friend, Livs – Olivia – a short, freckly girl who was chewing gum at three-hundred miles an hour – nodded and said, 'Yeah. Love it. That's art. You'll get an A-star for that.'

Evie wondered why she was feeling so awkward. Why was it so much easier to stand up to an actual deadly killer African *LIONESS* than to an annoying, spoilt twelve-year-old?

Leonora was right there now. She leaned in, close to Evie's face. 'Aren't you going to say something?'

Ramesh tutted at Leonora. 'You're just jealous that you're no longer the most famous girl in school.'

'Yeah,' sighed Leonora sarcastically. 'That must be it. Jealous. Got it. Well done, Sherlock Holmes.'

Then Evie saw something flying through the sky. Something small.

She recognised the wings instantly. They were the wings of a sparrow.

It wasn't just *any* sparrow, either.

It was Beak.

Evie could feel his thoughts enter her mind as he danced and darted in the air overhead. Evie closed her eyes to focus better.

'Are you all right, Evie?' asked the bird.

'Yes.'

'Are you sure?'

There was never any point lying to Beak. Beak always knew the truth.

'No, Beak. I'm not all right.'

'Do you want that girl to leave you alone?'

'Yes. But I don't think that's going to happen.'

Evie could hear Anoushka laughing. 'Oh man, look at her with her eyes closed! What's she doing? Yoga?'

Ramesh, meanwhile, was looked up at the bird. He knew something was going on.

'Wait there,' said Beak. 'I'll get my friends. They're right there, in that tree.'

Evie opened her eyes and looked up and saw the sparrow had disappeared.

167

Leonora was waving her hand in front of Evie's face.

'Hell-ooo! Are you listening? Is anyone home? Earth to Evie . . .'

Evie and Ramesh kept watching as a whole flock of sparrows came into view. She could hear Beak.

'Not the ones sitting down . . . the others.'

Then Anoushka grabbed Evie's hair and yanked it.

'Hey, Lion Girl. She *saaaid*, Are. You. **LISTENING?**'

Anoushka let go, and Evie stared at her former best friend and tried to pretend Leonora was no scarier than a lioness. 'No. Actually, I'm not,' she said.

Leonora and her friends were shocked by this answer and the sudden lack of fear in Evie's eyes. But not as shocked as they were a second later, when Beak reappeared with all the sparrows from the tree – Evie reckoned there were at

168

SPLAT!

SPLAT!

SPLAT!

SPLAT!

SPLAT!

least thirty of them – circling over their heads. They flew fast. Closer and closer.

Leonora stared up at the sky and—

SPLAT!

A splodge of sticky speckled sparrow poo landed right in the middle of her forehead.

'Ugh! Oh my god, it just pooed on me!'

SPLAT!

Another sparrow poo-splat, this time in her hair.

SPLAT! SPLAT! SPLAT! SPLAT! SPLAT!

Leonora was now covered in sparrow poo. And not just Leonora. Her friends as well.

'Aaaagh! Those evil birds!' spluttered Olivia.

'Ugh!' said one of the other girls. 'It's in my hair!'

Evie arrowed a message into Beak's brain. 'Okay, Beak. Thank you. That should do it.'

Beak circled overhead. 'Are you sure?'

'Yes. Sure.'

Beak called his friends away.

And now the whole schoolyard was watching. A massive crowd was gathering, then Leonora spotted a few people with their phones out, filming the whole thing. It was the first time this week that the news had been anything other than Evie and the lion.

170

'PUT THOSE PHONES AWAY! STOP FILMING!' Leonora screamed, bright red with rage.

Evie then felt her own phone buzz in her pocket. She looked at it and saw her dad had just sent a text message. It said:

I'll pick you up from school. To be safe.
Dad. X

Evie put the phone away.

Ramesh stopped staring at Leonora and looked at Evie and gave her a little smile and a nod. And even though Ramesh wasn't a sparrow or a lion Evie knew what the look meant. It meant: 'I believe you.' And she was grateful.

It felt nice to be understood.

The Girl Who Talks to Lions

Evie waited at the school gates for her dad to pick her up.

All the kids had left now, and her dad still hadn't arrived.

A man with a springer spaniel walked by. It was the totally mad and friendly dog she had seen a few weeks ago. The one with the stern owner. As it had done before, it began to sniff and pant and wag enthusiastically in Evie's direction.

'Hello. Hello. Hello. How are you?' he said. 'Life is good. Life is good. Despite everything. Life is good. Like me. Like me. Do you like me?'

Again, the dog's owner yanked him back hard on the lead. 'Behave, Murdoch!'

'Agh! I really do wish he knew how much that hurt.'

Evie couldn't help herself. 'I don't think he likes that,' she said.

The man looked at her with disgust. 'What?'

'He doesn't like it when you pull on the lead.'

He leaned in closer. 'It's *you*, isn't it? That stupid girl who thinks she can talk to lions.'

'What?'

'I've just read about it. In the *Lofting Evening Post*.'

He waved a newspaper in front of her, and then showed her the front page.

There was the headline, in big bold letters, with Evie's school photo next to it:

THE GIRL WHO TALKS TO LIONS

'Oh no,' Evie whispered. It was her seventy-second 'oh no' of the day.

The man walked away.

Evie looked at her watch. It was now a quarter past four. She sent her dad a text.

Am outside school. Are you still picking me up? X

No answer. So she sent another.

Dad, where are you? X

173

She even asked him in Spanish.

Papá ¿Dónde estás? x

Then another.

Dad?

Then one more.

Don't bother picking me up. Am walking home. Hope all okay. X

And so she did just that.

But she had a terrible feeling in her stomach. On her way home, Evie saw even more posters for missing pets. There seemed to be one on every lamp-post.

As she passed Leonora's house she saw Mrs Brightside being filmed by Mr Brightside, outside, on the pavement in front of their driveway. Daisy Brightside was talking into the camera.

'I have some **REALLY SAD** news,' she said, through dramatic sobs. 'Really, really, really, really **SAD**. Our beloved baby fluffball Bibi is missing. And the only explanation is that somebody stole her.' Then she waved at her husband.

'What is it, babe?' asked Mr Brightside, who was wearing a tight T-shirt to show off his fake-tanned muscles.

'I think we'll have to do that again, Jamie. My hair's too messy. I look like an ordinary . . . *person*.'

Evie felt her heart quicken. She remembered what that very same Maltese terrier had been saying through the window that morning.

He's coming . . .

She felt that whoever had stolen Bibi probably had something to do with all the other missing animals, too. That many pets simply didn't go missing in the space of a day, unless it was part of the same crime.

She went up to Leonora's mum between takes. 'Hi. Um, it's me. Evie. I used to be friends with Leonora.'

Mrs Brightside looked at Evie and gave a big fake smile. 'Oh yes! Lion Girl! Now, could you please tell me what happened at school today? Leonora came home *stinking* of **POO** and in a terrible state . . .'

'Um. I don't know. I'm just . . . I'm sorry to hear about what happened to your dog. I think something might be going on . . . You see, there are a lot of other missing animals—'

'I'm so sorry,' said Mrs Brightside, her smile even wider, as she looked at her watch. 'We have to get on with filming. We want this wrapped for seven to maximise the views . . .'

Evie felt a strange sensation, as if she was sinking into the pavement. She nodded, and ran away. Fast, towards home.

She suddenly knew something was wrong. Her dad was never late for anything. And if he was running late he would have told her.

In ten minutes she was home. But she couldn't get *in* because her dad wasn't answering and she didn't have a key. She noticed a snail crawling along the ground and then remembered her dad left a key under the flowerpot by the front door, so she found that.

Once inside she shouted, 'Dad? Dad?'

But there was no reply.

The Snail

It didn't take long to search the house.

And then the garage.

But her dad wasn't anywhere. Not downstairs, not upstairs, not with his broken furniture. Nowhere.

'Dad? Dad? Are you here?'

Evie panicked. In the kitchen she saw a half-eaten peanut butter sandwich on a plate. Her dad always had a peanut butter sandwich for lunch, but Evie had never – in her whole life – seen her dad not finish a peanut butter sandwich.

'Weird,' she said aloud, as her heart drummed fast inside her. 'Weird, weird, weird.'

She stepped outside the front door and looked all around. His car was still there.

Then amid her panic she remembered the snail.

Now, of course, she knew that snails were gastropods, and she remembered what had happened the last time she had encountered a gastropod. She had collapsed asleep on Granny Flora's lawn.

177

But she also knew that the snail had probably been around the front of the house all day. And it would have answers. And right then, Evie needed answers.

She crouched down to try to contact the shelled creature.

Its two tentacles leaned forward. Evie knew this was where snails have their eyes. On the tips of their tentacles.

She focused hard.

'Can you see me?'

Evie stared at the snail. She started to let the world slip away, as Granny Flora had instructed.

'Snail,' she thought, 'can you understand me? Can you hear my thoughts? I am here. I am human. The big creature looking down at you.'

The snail made no sign whatsoever of having heard Evie's thoughts. It just kept on snailing along. Evie knew she wouldn't be able to ask

questions. She'd have to go further. She'd have to try and find the dawa. She'd have to go right inside the snail's slow and sleepy mind.

She closed her eyes.

She tried to find the darkest spot behind her closed eyelids and she focused all her mind on it. She felt a slow kind of calmness. She was incredibly sleepy now, but she kept on.

With the lion, the dawa had manifested itself as a wind, but with the snail it was different. It was *weight*.

She felt a kind of heaviness throughout her whole body. She tried desperately to stay awake. It was going to be hard. She hadn't even reached the dawa with the slug and she had collapsed on the lawn.

But she had more adrenaline in her now. More determination. She kept trying.

And then the darkness bloomed into sudden light and, all of a sudden, she saw what the snail was seeing.

She saw her own giant human face, closing its eyes.

She began to feel the snail's living energy, which – being a snail – was a kind of deep and slow energy. She felt a dull vibration throughout her body.

179

The snail was worried.

She found memories of a bird — a dark bird, a crow — landing inches away from the snail.

Evie's body was feeling heavier as she — via the snail — tried to remember. And then she saw something.

Legs.

Human legs.

In khaki trousers.

A man, knocking on the door.

And then her father answering.

Evie couldn't hear what they were saying, because the snail hadn't heard anything. Because the snail was a snail.

She couldn't see the man's face. At first she couldn't see anything but the man's trousers. Khaki. The kind you'd wear in a war. Or a jungle.

But then she caught a glimpse of the man's right hand. It was a very noticeable hand. It had a ring on it. A round sovereign ring. But that wasn't the noticeable bit. The noticeable bit was the tattoo. There was a black tattoo of a coiled snake with its jaws open and its tongue out. It was a very scary-looking tattoo. But the scariest thing about it wasn't the way it looked

180

– though that was bad enough. The scariest bit was that she felt she recognised it from her dream.

And then she saw the man – or his legs – disappear inside the house. With her father. The door closed. She tried to find a later memory. Of the man and her father leaving the house. But she was getting more and more exhausted because a snail's memories are very weak and you have to do a lot of wading to find them.

But then, at the point of near collapse, she saw it.

The door opening and her father walking out in front of the man, and out of the snail's view. She noticed her father was still wearing his slippers and pyjamas. This wasn't that unusual. And then everything went black.

The next thing Evie knew she was lying on the path, opening her eyes, feeling sluggish. Or snailish. Which was just as bad.

She got slowly to her feet and tried to think.

This is what she knew.

Her dad was missing.

He had left at around lunchtime, during his sandwich.

There had been no visible struggle.

He had left with a man in khaki trousers.
A man with a tattoo on his right hand.
A man who she now recognised as Mortimer
J Mortimer.

Thirty-five Minutes

Evie went back into the house.

She paced around, trying to look for more clues, but there was nothing except the sandwich. She phoned 999 to tell the police her father was missing.

'And how long has your father been missing?' asked the policewoman on the end of the line.

'Um. I don't know exactly. But I think since lunch.'

'Okay.' The policewoman sounded bored. 'When did you know for sure that he wasn't at home?'

Evie looked at her watch. 'Thirty-five minutes ago.'

She heard the policewoman sigh. '*Riiiight.* Well, I'm sure there's a perfectly innocent explanation.'

'No. I just know something's happened to him. He left half his sandwich. He's never left an uneaten sandwich in his life.'

The policewoman sighed again. The

sandwich thing clearly hadn't impressed her. 'A sandwich?'

'Yes. **A PEANUT BUTTER** sandwich.'

'Is this a prank call?'

'No. I promise you.'

'Half-eaten sandwiches aren't evidence. Even ones containing peanut butter.'

'They might be!'

'Of what? Indigestion?'

Evie was feeling very frustrated now. 'He was meant to pick me up from school but he wasn't there. Aren't you going to launch an investigation?'

'Into a half-eaten sandwich? No. We have quite a lot of missing animals to deal with.'

'Yes, I know. I think this is related.'

'You think an animal ate the sandwich?'

'You don't understand,' said Evie. 'I think he's been . . . kidnapped. You see, I saw him leave with a man. A man with khaki trousers and a snake tattoo on his hand. And he wouldn't have gone anywhere without telling me. I just know he—'

'You saw him leave?'

'Yes. But, you see – the thing is, there was a snail.'

The police officer groaned wearily. 'A snail?'

184

'Yes. A snail. Outside. Near the flowerpot. And the thing is, I have this . . . err, this *gift*. The official name for it is the Talent. I can kind of enter the minds of animals.'

'Oh,' sighed the officer. 'I see. You should have just told me that at the start.'

'You see,' continued Evie breathlessly, 'I think that might be why my dad's in danger. I think that might have something to do with why he is missing . . . Because there is a man called Mortimer J Mortimer, who killed my mother by taking over the mind of a Brazilian wandering spider, and—'

It was at that precise point that Evie realised the policewoman had put the phone down on her.

This was hopeless.

If she wanted to find her dad before it was too late, she was on her own. Or was she? At that moment she noticed a bag of liquorice on the kitchen bench. Granny Flora.

So she ran. She ran all the way to Granny Flora's bungalow. When she got there she was out of breath. But Granny Flora wasn't there.

Nor was anyone else, except Plato, who was outside, eating a piece of asparagus Granny Flora had left out for him. This was strange.

She had never seen Plato not at Granny Flora's side.

'Plato,' Evie said. And then she said the same thing with her mind. 'Plato.'

And Plato just chewed slowly on the asparagus.

'Plato, where is Granny Flora?'

No response.

She stared at him. Then she closed her eyes. She thought about arrows. She tried to reach the dawa. But nothing. Plato was impenetrable.

But no. If Granny Flora could do it, so could she. It had to be possible.

'Plato, Granny Flora is in trouble. You need to tell me what you know. What is going on?'

She thought of what Granny Flora had said, that day with Marmalade. She heard her voice echo in her mind.

You need to make it INEVITABLE. You need not a shadow of doubt. You need to become him. Don't just understand the animal, be the animal.

A thought came to Evie. As Granny Flora never went anywhere without Plato, she might have known she was going to be taken. Maybe she had left Plato on purpose. Maybe Plato had told Granny Flora where to go.

She knew that she couldn't simply ask Plato a question. She had to go all the way inside

186

his mind. She tried again to reach into the dawa. But it seemed impossible.

She thought of something else Granny Flora had said.

Everything is impossible until you can do it.

We are all linked. Life is life. Everything connects.

'Everything connects,' whispered Evie. 'Everything connects, everything connects . . .'

In the darkness of her closed eyes she concentrated right on the darkest part. She felt a coldness from inside her body. As if all her blood was suddenly starting to cool to the level of a reptile. She could hardly breathe. She knew if she opened her eyes she would feel instantly better, but she had to keep on, heading deeper into the dawa until she was there. And then in the darkness she slipped inside Plato's mind. She saw trees. Many, many trees. And there was Granny Flora. Her face looked troubled.

'The forest,' came the thought.

A strong, mysterious, all-knowing thought.

The thought of a bearded dragon.

'You must go to the woods. There, you will find all that you seek. He knows you will come. But there, your past will free your future . . .'

Evie opened her eyes. She could breathe again. Her body warmed back into life.

She stared at the green lizard, still chewing on his asparagus. He looked up and stared at her for a moment, with eyes that seemed older than time.

'Thank you, Plato,' she said.

And then Evie started to run to Lofting Wood.

The Stag

She ran until her lungs were bursting. She ran and didn't stop, passing hundreds of missing posters. She ran even when she saw Scruff near the bins outside the back of Sun Palace, the Cantonese restaurant.

Scruff – along with Plato – seemed to be among the few animals who hadn't gone missing. 'Hello, Evie! Where are you going?'

'Sorry, Scruff!' she thought back. 'No time to answer!'

'Are you going where all the others are going?' said Scruff. 'Wow, weird times.'

Evie passed her old primary school. And kept running, to the field where she had let Kahlo the rabbit free, and she carried on, up the gentle slope, with farmland and the zoo to her left and Lofting town and its church with its witch-hat steeple to her right, towards the forest. Towards Lofting Wood. By the time she got there, it was almost dark. And totally empty. No one ever went to Lofting Wood because they were always inside working or watching telly or playing video games. Even the dog-walkers went to the park in town, near the church.

The trees stood against the sky like a strange army, waiting for battle.

As soon as she was in there, in the forest itself, she noticed holes in the ground. Rabbit holes.

Of course!

She remembered. This was the place Kahlo had called the Forest of Holes.

A male deer stopped ahead of her through the trees. Its antlers spread up and back and wide like wild beautiful branches were growing out of its head. An average-sized male deer was called a buck, but Evie knew this was bigger than average and so it was a stag. There was still just enough light in the sky for Evie to realise he was one of the most beautiful animals she had ever seen.

'What are you?'

'I'm Evie. I'm a human. But I'm not going to hurt you.'

'You are not of the forest.'

'What?'

The stag didn't seem at all perturbed that

190

Evie understood him, and that she was communicating with him.

'There are two kinds of thing. Things of the forest. And things not of the forest. And you are not of the forest.'

Evie could sense its proud mind. It felt strong, as rooted as the oak and sycamore trees around it.

'You are right. I am not of the forest. And I will leave the forest. I just need to find someone. Maybe you could help me . . . I'm looking for my dad. He's like me. But taller. And a man.'

'I don't know. But there are a lot of cats. And dogs. And other things not of the forest.'

'Where?'

The stag tilted its head. 'They went that way . . . I will show you. Follow me.'

So Evie followed this giant stag deeper and deeper through the trees.

'This way, this way . . .' the stag kept saying. 'You're getting closer . . .'

And then Evie saw them all, in a low clearing. Animals of every shape and size. Silhouettes of all the missing pets. Dogs, cats, hamsters, parrots, even a few horses. All standing totally still – and obedient. She looked around for her dad, or Granny Flora, or for Mortimer J Mortimer himself.

'This way . . .' the stag kept saying. 'This way . . . this way . . . this—'

She heard a voice she recognised.

'Evie! No! Don't listen to the stag!'

It was Granny Flora. Evie turned and saw her, tied to an oak tree.

'Granny?'

Evie began to run towards her.

'No!' Granny Flora shouted.

But it was too late.

In between leaping with one foot and

192

landing on the other, she looked down at the leafy ground and saw, to her shock, there was no ground at all. Her foot kept falling, and her body too, and she fell and fell and fell. Until **BOOM!** She hit hard cold earth at the bottom of a large hole.

In the Hole

It was even darker in the hole than it had been out of it. But she heard her dad's voice.

'Evie, are you okay?' He came closer to her. He put an arm on her shoulder.

'Dad!' She hugged him. 'Oh, Dad. What's going on?'

'It's him. It's Mortimer. He's got us both here. He came for me earlier. I had to go with him. He said if I didn't he'd hurt you. But he knew you would follow . . .'

Evie looked up and saw the stag's head leaning over the hole above her. 'I have followed my command . . .'

And then Evie's dad quickly explained, 'He's mind-controlling all the animals in Lofting. Most of them, anyway.'

'The dawa . . .'

'Yes. Your mum told me he was the master of it. He can find the dawa within any animal. And then control them completely. Not just one at a time, either. But I never realised he was this powerful.'

194

Evie got to her feet. 'Is there a way to climb out?'

'No. It's too deep. It's amazing what a few mind-controlled dogs can do.'

'Dogs?' wondered Evie.

And then she saw them. Sitting in the base of the hole. Four dogs. An Alsatian, a Labradoodle (a Labradoodle Evie had seen on a poster earlier that day), a Rottweiler and Bibi, Leonora's Maltese terrier. They were all staring straight at them, totally brainwashed.

'And he's got Granny Flora tied to a tree,' Evie's dad said.

'I know. I saw. Poor Granny Flora.' She was scared to ask the next thing, but she asked it anyway. 'Where is he?'

Evie's dad didn't have time to respond, as there was a voice from above. A smooth, deep voice like poison and velvet. A voice she'd heard somewhere before.

'Oh,' the voice said. 'I'm *everywhere.*'

Evie looked up and there, where the stag had been only moments before, was a man illuminated by the moonlight. A tall man with a black moustache wearing what looked like a thin scarf around his neck. Evie felt cold just looking at him. It was Mortimer J Mortimer himself. It took Evie a moment to realise that the scarf wasn't a scarf at all. It was a snake.

'You killed my mum,' Evie said, in a scared mumble, but her dad touched her arm as if to say, 'Don't aggravate him.'

'So, here we are, Isabella. All three of you. The hat-trick.'

'My name is Evie.'

Mortimer ignored her. 'All I need now is that stupid little boy . . . But that can wait till tomorrow.'

'Please,' said Evie's dad. 'Do anything you want to me. But don't hurt Evie. Don't hurt Flora.'

Mortimer laughed. It was a wild laugh that filled the sky itself. 'Oh, Mr Navarro. Santiago, if I may. You overestimate your importance. I am here for them. The ones with the Talent . . . Now, obviously, their Talent isn't quite a match for mine. It never could be. But it would be very useful if we were all on the same team.'

Evie felt sick at the idea. 'You killed my mum.' Her voice trembled with anger. 'I could never be on your team.'

Mortimer looked down at her, as the snake he was wearing slithered restlessly.

'Your mother didn't see the big picture. You see, she thought she was saving animals . . .

198

But really, she was placing them in grave danger. Animals can't protect themselves with humans around. It's a losing battle. We're the top of the food chain. Come on, Evie, think about it. Look at what we've done to the world. Look at how many miraculous species we humans have made extinct. The woolly mammoth. The dodo. The Tasmanian tiger. The black rhino. And literally thousands and thousands more. I'm not the only monster, Evie. We're all monsters. And we're getting worse. Climate change? Rising sea levels? Turning the ocean to acid and plastic? That's not the fault of jellyfish, is it?'

Although her dad was trying to tell her to be quiet, Evie couldn't help herself. 'You worked for the loggers! The criminal loggers who were chopping down the Amazon. They paid you to kill my mother. Because she was trying to stop them.'

'You need to see the bigger picture, Evie. Yes, I made a lot of money. But this means now I never have to work another day in my life. I can devote myself to good causes.'

Evie stepped forward in the hole, away from her dad, and winced with pain. She had hurt her ankle during the fall. The same ankle she

199

had hurt at the zoo. But she had bigger things to think about.

'Good causes? Like murder?'

'No, like animal preservation. And there's only one way to do that . . .'

'How?'

'Well, we get the animals to take over. I've been working on it for a long while. I've been trying to recruit people. People like you. People like your grandmother. And I must admit, it hasn't been entirely successful so far. I even tried to recruit your mother, back in the day. Did you know that?'

'So when people turn you down, you kill them?'

Even in the dark she could see Mortimer smirk as he leaned over the hole. 'That's quite a negative way of looking at it. But yes, essentially correct. I have to get rid of those that stand in the way of my vision. Because, well, it is a great vision. It is a vision of a better world.'

'A better world?' spat Evie in disgust.

'Yes. One with the animals on top and the humans on the bottom. They just need guidance. *My* guidance. And maybe your guidance too. I understand from the lions at

200

the zoo that you are able to connect with the dawa. That is good. Your Talent can grow. Maybe one day you could be like me . . . But in the meantime, I must be in charge. And you could help me. You see, it is a very big plan. The largest revolution in history. The animals taking over the humans. So that's the choice. You're either with me, or you're against me.' Mortimer checked his watch. 'I have a busy night ahead. And then tomorrow, we could take over the world. Starting with this disgusting little town.'

'I don't want to take over the world. I just want to be free.'

Mortimer smiled. 'It's the same thing. Now, I'll leave you to decide. Join me and live. Or . . . a little bite from my snake friend here. The choice is yours. Back in a while . . . Toodle-pip.'

And with that Mortimer, and his snake, disappeared.

'And for a moment Evie heard nothing except the heavy beating of her heart.'

201

The Human Who Is Good

Evie's dad looked at her with wild, desperate eyes. 'I don't know what he is going to do with me. But you and Granny Flora can be free. All you have to do is agree to work for him.'

Evie looked at her phone, thinking she could call Ramesh. Or try the police again. But there was no signal. And none on her dad's either. 'But that's not freedom,' she said. 'He wants to wage war on humans. He doesn't care about animals. He cares about *controlling* them. He cares about power.'

Her dad nodded. 'He's going to kill people. That's what he is going to do. Rumour had it that he once used a pack of jaguars to help him rob a bank in Brazil. The last thing he wants is to free animals; he wants to imprison them. They're his slaves.'

Evie thought, as she looked up from the bottom of the hole at the night sky, 'Well, I'm not going to be his slave.'

Then she noticed the dogs again. The dogs

in the hole. The Labrador, the Rottweiler, the Alsatian and poor little Bibi. The dogs whose minds she hadn't been able to read because they were under the control of Mortimer. They were now all lying on the ground, fast asleep.

'They must be exhausted,' Evie's dad noted. 'From all that digging. He probably told them to sleep only when they'd finished.'

Evie jumped up and tried to grab hold of a root that was sticking out of the side of the hole. But she lost her grip and fell back down.

'There's no way out that way. I've tried.'

Evie sat down, her head leaning against the dirt wall.

'I'm sorry,' she said. 'You were right. We should have got out of Lofting when we had the chance.'

Her dad shrugged. 'He'd have found us. He'd have made sure of it. It's not your fault.'

Then Evie thought of Granny Flora. 'Are you all right, Granny?' she shouted out loud.

'Oh yes,' came a faraway voice, with a reassuring chuckle. 'Never been better. Just tied to a tree in the middle of a forest.'

Then, to her dad, Evie whispered, 'Maybe Granny Flora can use her Talent. Maybe she can turn the animals against him and onto our

203

side. Maybe she could find a bird – a woodpecker – to peck through her rope.'

'She's good, Evie, but I don't think she's that good. He'll have thought of that. And even if she got free, all the other animals up there – the dogs and horses and the deer and whatever else – they are his now. They act as one. They are all part of his mind.' He pointed to the four sleeping dogs. 'And most of them won't be asleep.'

Evie let out a small growl of frustration as she tapped her head against the side of the hole.

But then she heard something. A thought.

'Digging is fun,' went the thought. 'Digging is joy. Digging and hopping make worries fade away. Nothing beats digging and hopping. Down in the dark. Dig dig dig. Hop hop hop.'

Evie recognised the voice. The thought-voice.

'Kahlo,' she whispered.

'What?' asked her confused dad.

'Nothing,' she said. Then, with closed eyes, she tried to concentrate and send silent thought-messages.

'Kahlo? Can you hear me? It's me, Evie. The school girl who set you free from the hutch. Last year.'

Evie waited.

204

There was nothing at first . . .

And then: 'Evie?'

'Yes.'

'I remember you. Of course I remember you! You were my liberator. The Human Who Is Good. I didn't know you liked digging at night too?'

'I, um, don't.'

'Night digging is the best! I didn't know humans liked it, too . . . The freedom of going deep into something. Of somewhere *un-dug*. Knowing you are the first rabbit ever to be in that particular place. Wow. It's the best life has to offer.'

'Kahlo, listen. I wasn't digging!'

'Well, how are you down here, then?'

Evie explained what was happening. The thoughts burst out of her in one gush.

'Oh my goodness,' said Kahlo. 'That doesn't sound very good. I must remember to stay underground. He must have overlooked us. That's the great thing about being a rabbit. Everyone always overlooks us.'

'Now,' thought Evie, 'do you remember when I set you free? You said you'd repay the favour if ever I asked you?'

'Uh-huh. Oh yes. I remember. Of course. I

205

remember everything about that day. I have told everyone in the warren that story a hundred times. The whole colony thinks you're a hero. The Human Who Is Good.' Then Evie heard Kahlo speak to someone else. 'Hey, Fury. Guess who's in the neighbourhood? It's the Human Who Is Good.'

Evie's dad was looking at her suspiciously. 'Evie, what are you doing? You're not using the Talent, are you?'

'Dad, if there was ever a time to use it, I think it is now, don't you?'

Her dad couldn't say much to that.

'Wherever Mortimer's gone, he's going to be back soon. So we have to act fast, Dad.'

Then Evie switched her mind back to Kahlo. 'Now,' she said, 'I have a plan. But I'm going to need you and all your friends to help . . .'

'That's fine.'

Evie tried to work something out. 'Kahlo, how many rabbits are there in your colony?'

'Forty-three,' said Kahlo. 'If you count Colin. But we could get the other colonies to help. That would make four hundred of us. The forgotten, the overlooked, the underground . . . All here at the service of the Human Who Is Good!'

The Plan

It was a simple plan, but the rabbits had to work fast.

Which was okay, because rabbits were the fastest and hardest and most tireless workers in the world when they put their minds to it.

The idea was that they dig a rabbit tunnel from the hole where Evie and her dad were trapped to the very edge of the forest. It had to be large enough for two humans to fit through. And it had to be far enough to get them beyond all the animals above ground that were awake and under his control. And so the rabbits got to work, doing what they did best. Digging and burrowing. Side by side, and even on top of each other.

The part of the plan that was a bit more complicated was the part about Granny Flora. They couldn't leave Granny Flora tied to a tree, obviously. But also, Evie and her dad couldn't help her while they were still stuck at the bottom of a hole.

So, Evie asked Kahlo if it was possible to

make one part of the tunnel reach right below Granny Flora's feet, so that Evie or her dad could pop up and untie the rope or cut it with the sharp stone that Evie's dad had found and was now holding in his hands.

And, well, that's exactly what happened.

The rabbits from five separate colonies joined forces, and they made fast progress. They worked out which tree Granny Flora was tied to, and once they had made it through, and made the tunnel big enough, Evie – who was smaller than her dad – was chosen to head out with the stone and cut the rope.

'Oh my! Good work, buttercup!' Granny Flora told Evie. 'But be quick . . . *Look!*'

Evie looked.

Hundreds of cats and dogs and horses and a stag and guinea pigs and hamsters and a – a bull – were now all heading towards her, with the same blank zombified look on their faces.

Evie knew that the thing to do with bulls was to stay as still as possible, as bulls reacted to movement (not the colour red, as some people thought, because bulls are colour-blind).

Evie felt a cat jump and claw her leg. And then another, and another, and another, and another. She started shaking them off.

210

Then she saw a ginger tabby.

'Marmalade? Marmalade!' said Evie.

'Must stop them!' said Marmalade, scratching her leg. 'Must kill them!'

'Marmalade, snap out of it. You are being mind-controlled. You all are.'

A hamster bit her ankle. She tried to use the Talent. But it was no good. Every creature above ground seemed entirely at the service of Mortimer J Mortimer, and he must have instructed all of them to stop them from escaping.

It was the bull Evie was most worried about, though. It had studied exactly where they were, worked out the right angle, and now its dark silhouette was galloping fast towards her and Granny Flora, like a hulking shadow made of muscle.

'I WILL DESTROY YOU!' thundered the bull as it charged closer.

The Roots of the Tree

Feeling desperate, Evie struggled with the rope, scraping it with the sharp stone as fast as she could until she cut Granny Flora free.

And then Granny Flora stood in front of the tree and stared at the bull, trying to break it out of its spell, but Evie could see there was no way. Mortimer's control over the animals was too strong.

So she tackled Granny Flora into the rabbit hole.

'Sorry, Granny,' said Evie, as they landed in the steeply sloping muddy darkness. 'I was just trying to keep you alive!'

'That's okay,' said Granny Flora. 'It's only my knee. And I'm getting a new one in March. I've already booked the appointment!'

They felt scrapey branches on their heads.

'What's that?' wondered Evie.

'It's the roots of the tree,' said her dad. 'It's no longer fixed in the ground because of all the digging.'

212

And then . . .

They heard the bull charge with such a crunching **WHACK** into the tree that it became unrooted. A moment later and the tree landed with an earthquaking **THUD**.

The tree was now almost completely blocking the entrance to the rabbit hole. Only hamsters and mice were getting through.

'Must kill!' thought the mice.

'Must stop them!' said a pair of hamsters with their minds at once.

'Must destroy!' thought a guinea pig, nibbling furiously on Evie's shoelace.

'Quick!' said Kahlo to the humans. 'This way! Follow us.'

Some of the rabbits lagged behind to block the path of all the small furry creatures.

So the three humans, on their hands and knees, crawled through the earth. As they went, whole lines – whole *squadrons* – of rabbits burrowed in front of them in the dark, in semi-circles, their front paws working like crazy, spraying dirt between their back legs.

'Oh my,' said Granny Flora. 'It's darker than liquorice down here.'

They passed the occasional earthworm ('Hey, be careful!') and had to watch out for sharp

213

bits of grit and stone. Also, it wasn't very easy to breathe, so they kept their mouths tight shut.

It was hard to tell how long they burrowed but eventually the rabbits started to aim their tunnel upwards. And finally they glimpsed starlight, and felt grass, and smelled the cool air of the night. And freedom.

As Evie climbed out of the tunnel she communicated a few words telepathically. 'Thank you, Kahlo. Thank you, everyone. You have been so helpful. I will never forget this. None of us will.'

'Goodbye,' said the rabbits, all at once. 'We shall never forget this night we worked together for the Human Who Is Good.'

And the rabbits disappeared, heading back deep under the ground.

Evie helped Granny Flora and then her dad climb out of the tunnel. They all stepped out, spitting earth from their mouths. Evie's dad brushed the dirt from his beard.

For a moment, it seemed as if they were safe.

The forest was behind them. And Evie's primary school and the rest of Lofting was there in front of them. The whole town was still and quiet, as it always was at night.

'What now?' Evie wondered, shaking the dirt off her.

'Well, I don't think we should even try to go home,' her dad suggested. 'We should probably just get a taxi and get as far out of Lofting as possible. Before Mortimer comes back . . .'

Granny Flora seemed troubled. 'No. Something is wrong. I can feel it.'

And then she saw it. *Them.*

They all did.

A procession of animals heading over the farmland in the east. And they weren't farm animals either.

Evie looked at her phone. There was a signal now and a text from Ramesh.

OMG – someone broke into the zoo! No joke. Repeat – no joke. THE ANIMALS ARE MISSING!!!!!!!!!!

The Apprentice

Evie stared at the text.

There weren't any emojis. Which showed how serious Ramesh found this news.

And looking away from her phone, even in the dark, Evie could see them getting closer and closer to her and her dad and Granny Flora and to the forest.

Animals of every size.

The tall necks of giraffes.

The stout bodies of elephants.

The heavy muscular shoulders of gorillas.

Maybe even some reptiles, slinking through the grass.

And there, front and centre, was Mortimer J Mortimer, flanked by the four lions. He was holding a child's hand.

'Oh no,' said Evie's dad. 'He's got the boy.'

'Well, well, well,' said Mortimer, raising a hand for the animals to halt as he and little Sam came closer. 'I must say, I underestimated you.'

He began to clap slowly, as the snake adorning his neck raised its head. Evie noted the snake tattoo on his hand and absently wondered if it was the same creature.

'So, I think this tells me everything I need to know about your decision,' sighed Mortimer. 'I must say, I'm disappointed. Very disappointed indeed.'

'Hello, Evie!' said Sam, smiling cheerfully, as if there was nothing at all weird about being a six-year-old boy standing in a forest at ten o'clock at night, surrounded by elephants and lions.

'Hi Sam,' said Evie, in a ghostly voice. 'Where's your mum?'

'Oh, she's asleep. But a cat told me to sneak out and meet Mr Mortimer! He's going to help me talk to all the animals!'

'I certainly am,' smiled Mortimer. 'You're my apprentice now.'

'App-ren-tice,' said Sam, liking the sound of this new word.

'You've got to stop this, Mortimer,' hissed Granny Flora.

He nodded in mock agreement. 'You are absolutely right. I have to stop this. I have to stop this . . . And by *this*, I clearly mean *you*.

217

You three. You are a serious hindrance to the revolution. Wouldn't you say, Leaf?'

Leaf was the name of the snake around Mortimer's neck.

Evie could see the snake clearly now, under the moonlight. It was a plump vivid-green emerald tree boa.

'Me and Leaf go way back . . .' Mortimer explained to Evie. 'As far back as me and your mother, actually. Ecuador. I found him not too far from your old hut . . . He resisted my Talent a little. But we got there, eventually . . .'

Evie's dad stepped forward. 'Mortimer, please, leave us alone.'

'Don't be a spoil-sport,' Mortimer said. 'Let's play a game! It's called "Snake, lion or gorilla". Basically, you can choose how you want to die.' He pointed at Granny Flora. 'Oldest first. That seems fair. How do you want to die?'

'No,' said Evie's dad. 'Me first. Start with me. The one you knew first . . .'

Mortimer looked at him with pity. 'Poor old Santiago. Always too late, too weak, too pathetic to be the hero.' He then spoke to Granny Flora and repeated his question, slower this time. 'How. Do. You. Want. To. Die?'

220

Granny Flora chuckled darkly. She didn't want Evie to see she was scared. 'I am a mere eighty-two years old. I have no plans on dying any time soon, thank you very much.'

Mortimer cupped a hand to his ear, pretending he hadn't heard. 'Snake, you say? Well, that's convenient. Because Leaf right here—'

'No,' said Granny Flora, playing for time. 'I choose lion.' And she pointed at one of the male lions. The one with the largest mane. The one furthest away. The one who had stood behind the lioness at the zoo.

Mortimer beckoned the lion forward. The beast prowled closer. Its mane looked black in the dark.

It growled in front of the three of them.

Evie's dad noticed the look on his daughter's face. He could see she was focusing deeply on the snake around Mortimer's neck. He knew whatever she was attempting would take some time. So he decided to speak.

'You know,' he said to Mortimer. 'You're right. I'm too weak. I don't have any special Talent. I am just a man who tries to fix broken things. But I would rather be me. I would rather be able to do a little good than to do a whole world of bad.'

'Oh, are you giving me a lesson?' said Mortimer, fake-yawning. 'So inspiring.'

Evie's dad kept speaking, playing for time, as Evie stared at the boa constrictor. 'I knew the very first time I met you in Ecuador that you were bad news. But, somehow, I can't hate you. Even after all you've done. To be as evil as you are must be such a curse. To have no light in your soul. Nothing but darkness . . . You don't deserve hate. Hate is a waste of energy. You have a great Talent, but it means nothing. Because you have lost yourself. You are nothing. You are a black hole.'

'Shut your mouth, Santiago,' snapped Mortimer.

'No. No, I won't. Because you don't understand what you are doing. What is the point of all this? What happens? What will you do?'

'I . . . I don't want to be an app-ten-tice,' said Sam, pulling his hand out of Mortimer's. 'I want to go home.'

Evie, meanwhile, was concentrating very hard on trying to make the world disappear. She remembered what Plato had said. *You must go to the woods. There, you will find all*

222

that you seek. There, your past will free your future . . .

And so she kept staring at the snake around Mortimer's neck, as if it held the answer to everything.

Leaf's Revenge

As Evie stared, she had the strange sensation that she had seen him before. The snake. Leaf. *But where? But where? But where?*

The zoo. No, it wasn't there.

And then she had it.

The dream!

The dream of the green tree snake and the poison dart frog.

She still remembered that dream vividly. Because it hadn't been a dream at all. It had been something that had actually happened. To her. To the her she used to be. The little girl called Isabella Eva Navarro. Something that she kept remembering, night after night.

And she thought of it now.

Evie stared at the snake around Mortimer's shoulders. And then she closed her eyes as she remembered.

She tried to picture it all.

That brightly coloured, pretty blue and black frog. She had known this frog meant danger. But the

snake hadn't. The snake had been even younger than her. It hadn't known that the frog's skin was full of enough fatal poison to kill ten grown men.

She remembered urging the snake not to touch it.

'It will kill you.'

She remembered the snake stopping to look at her.

'If you even touch that frog, you will be dead,' Evie had said, with her mind.

She remembered feeling the snake inside her mind. She remembered hearing its thoughts. 'It looks plump. It looks tasty.'

'No,' Evie had told the snake firmly, pressing the thought into him. 'It is deadly. It is a poison dart frog. You are still a very young snake. You don't understand these things.'

'Why do you want to save me?' the snake – Leaf – had asked.

'Because I can.'

She had known that both the snake and the frog could kill her, but that hadn't meant she wanted them dead.

And then she remembered the important bit. Of the dream. Of the memory.

The snake had said: 'Thank you. You are a good human. Not like Mortimer.'

225

Mortimer. He had actually said the name.

'Who is Mortimer?'

'He is after me. He is trying to control me . . .'

As Evie kept her eyes closed, she felt the snake enter her thoughts.

'It was you!'

Evie opened her eyes and focused on the snake. Thought of the bow and arrow technique. 'Yes, it was me. I tried to save you. Unlike Mortimer, who tried to control you. Who is still trying to control you . . .'

And then she heard Mortimer's voice. 'What's going on? Leaf, what are you doing? You are under my control . . . You know you are under my control . . . I command you. I command everything. I have power over the dawa . . .'

The snake was moving around him now. *Coiling* around him. Around his neck and chest and stomach. Squeezing tighter. And tighter.

'You don't control me,' thought Leaf. 'No one controls me. You took me from my home, and I won't forgive you. You will not harm the girl who saved my life. I will not let you . . .'

'Leaf!' shouted Mortimer, his eyes bulging. 'Slide off me! Get off me and across the grass and constrict yourself around that old human woman! Now! Now! Nowaaaagh!'

226

Sam stared up in horror and fascination.

'Wow,' he whispered.

Mortimer tried to grab the snake and pull it away with his tattooed hands, but it was too late. Evie knew that Amazonian emerald tree boas could kill their prey quite quickly and it was really only a matter of seconds before Mortimer was lying still, dead, on the ground. Leaf sat there, still wrapped around his former master, making sure he wasn't going to move again.

And now, with Mortimer gone, the animals were freed from his control.

So Granny Flora used her Talent and reached out and touched the face of the lion who was about to kill her. And he sat down, like a pussy cat.

'Good boy,' said Granny Flora. 'There's a good boy.'

Within minutes there were cars and lorries and flashing lights heading towards them on the road at the bottom of the grass slope they were standing on. The four dogs who had dug the hole emerged from the tunnel the rabbits had dug, awake and no longer brainwashed.

The Maltese terrier yapped, 'What's going on? What's going on?'

'Bibi!' said Evie. 'You're you again.'

Then, out of one of the lorries – which had 'LOFTING ZOO' written on the side of it – stepped Ramesh and his mother, with her tranquiliser gun.

The police were there too. With lots of questions, obviously, but one of them was soon to be answered. They had footage of Mortimer, with Leaf around his neck, breaking into the zoo.

'Well,' said Granny Flora, 'I guess Plato was

228

right. We had to stay and solve this. And we did. Well, Evie did.'

Evie's dad agreed. 'Yes. Yes, she did. She's my star – *mi estrella* – and I should have followed her all along.'

'Thanks, Dad,' said Evie.

And there would be hugs and smiles and tears later. But right then, there were two people with the Talent who could help the animals get back to the zoo. So that is exactly what they did.

An Easy Decision

A few days later, Evie was at school with Ramesh.

They were sitting on their usual bench in the break between geography and art.

'Sorry about the zoo having to close down,' Evie told him.

Ramesh shrugged. 'Well, hardly your fault, is it? Anyway, Mum's pleased. She's got a new job. At the animal shelter. I haven't seen her this happy since, well, before Dad died . . .'

Evie smiled. 'Oh, cool. I might go there. See, I'm finally allowed to have a pet. Now Mortimer's dead and there's no reason to hide who I am any more.'

'What about that snake?' Ramesh asked. 'Or would that be a bit weird. With him being Mortimer's killer?'

'Leaf is on his way back to the Amazon. Back where he's happiest.'

Ramesh was about to say something else, but he saw Leonora walking over. On her own.

'Hey, Evie,' she said. 'I just wanted to say thank you. For helping find Bibi.'

Ramesh made wide eyes at Evie, but she did her best to be polite. 'Oh hey, no worries.'

'And I think you were right. You know. What you said. Last year. She doesn't like wearing some of the clothes I put her in. She likes her jumper, but that's about it . . .'

Another girl – older, tall, pink hair, Year Ten – came up holding a pen and a piece of paper. 'Hi, um, I wondered if I could have your autograph?'

Leonora turned and flicked her hair and gave her best vlogger smile. 'Of course. I'd be happy to.'

The girl was embarrassed. 'Actually, I meant Evie. The Lion Girl. It's not every week you find out someone at your school has special powers for real.'

'Oh sure,' said Leonora, laughing it off. 'Cool. Yeah. Cool. Of course. Yeah. Evie.'

This was happening quite a lot this week. People were treating Evie like a hero. Ever since footage had emerged of Evie and Granny Flora walking with the lions, and then an interview they had done on live TV with Plato and Beak, where Evie had read Beak's mind

233

(telling him to fly in a circle), and where the presenter had held an unseen card up for Plato, and Granny Flora had successfully said it was the ace of diamonds.

The Talent even had a technical name. It was called Ziegler Syndrome, apparently, after someone in Germany who'd had it a century ago. Now Mortimer J Mortimer was dead, people were talking about it more. One news report said there could be thousands of people worldwide with the condition. And the fact that Evie was also seen to be the one who had found everyone's missing pets meant the whole of Lofting was now on her side.

'Thanks,' said the Year Ten, staring at the signature as she walked away.

Leonora stood there awkwardly. 'My mum wondered if you wanted to appear in a video. You know. An episode. Of LIFE ON THE BRIGHTSIDE.'

Evie didn't really like the idea. But then she thought of something. 'That sounds great . . . Could we do it on ways to help save animals from extinction?'

Leonora shrugged, confused. 'Yeah. Sure. Why not?'

'That was fun,' said Ramesh, after Leonora

had gone. He mimed playing a guitar in triumph. 'Must be great, now you can be all out in the open.'

Evie thought of Beak. 'If you have wings, you might as well use them. That's what a little bird once told me.'

'That's a wise bird.'

Evie turned to Ramesh. 'Is the animal shelter open after school?'

And Ramesh said, 'Yeah. Till seven.'

'Right. Well, in that case, I'll see you there after school.'

So three hours later she was standing in Lofting Animal Shelter. With her dad and Granny Flora and Ramesh and his mum. Evie was staring at a dog she recognised. A tall brown and white dog who looked just as grubby as usual.

'Scruff? What are you doing here?'

'Life on the streets was starting to get to me. Too many cats. Too many cars. Too much hassle. And when everyone went missing it kind of freaked me out. So I handed myself in. Today, actually.'

'Wow,' thought Evie back at him. 'I see.'

'I was thinking . . .' said Scruff, sniffing awkwardly at nothing in particular.

235

'What were you thinking, Scruff?'

And Scruff stopped sniffing and stared up at her with eyes full of nervous happiness. 'Will you, possibly, maybe . . . take me home?'

Evie felt joy flood through her like a warm sunny day. She turned to her dad, who was raising his eyebrows doubtfully.

'This one, Dad. Please.'

'Are you sure?'

Evie had never been surer about anything. 'Absolutely.'

A Good Life

'Just close your eyes, Scruff,' Evie said, as she opened up the bottle of Pampered Paws 2-in-1 pet shampoo and conditioner.

Scruff was standing dripping wet in the shower, feeling very sorry for himself. 'This is so humiliating.'

'Scruff, please, close your eyes. I'm going to wash you now. You told me you were up for it.'

'Yes, I did. I did. But I didn't realise it was like this. This is disgusting.'

'It will stop you itching. You say you hate the itching. Come on. It's not that bad. Humans shower every day.'

'Well, humans are *insane*.'

Evie sighed and started to lather the shampoo onto Scruff's back.

Scruff wasn't impressed. Water dripped off his ears. 'I hate this stuff. And I hate water. Unless it's like a brown muddy puddle that I can roll around in. Because that feels like freedom.'

Evie felt guilty. 'Sorry, Scruff. I get that. But

you have scratched yourself quite badly with all the itching. And look, I can rinse it off now, and then we're done. I promise you. That's it now for another year. No more clean. I like you scruffy, too.'

She switched off the water and Scruff stepped out of the shower.

'Cold' was the only thought Evie could hear. 'Cold. Cold. Cold.'

Evie quickly wrapped a warm towel from the radiator around him and started to dry him.

'Oh, that's nice,' thought Scruff. 'I like these warm things.'

'Warm towels,' Evie explained. 'These are among the greatest human things.'

'I think I'm going to like it here,' said Scruff. 'You were always my favourite human.'

'Good,' said Evie. 'Because you're my favourite dog.'

A little later he was asleep in his basket, and Granny Flora was having her last cup of tea before Evie's dad drove her and Plato home.

Granny Flora smiled her soft twinkly-eyed smile at Evie, her teeth stained with tea and liquorice.

'Your real talent isn't talking to animals, Evie,'

238

she said after a while. 'It's kindness. That's what made you stronger than Mortimer in the end. Kindness is a boomerang. You throw it out and you get it back. You had done kind things in the world, and you had been rewarded with kindness in return.'

Evie smiled a little. 'Thanks, Granny.'

'Well, think about it. You were kind to that rabbit, and she then helped us escape. You helped that snake, and it saved your life. *Our* lives. You were kind to Scruff when you helped his poorly paw, and now he loves you. You were kind to Beak, and he pooped on your enemies . . .' She placed her cup of tea down and picked up Plato. 'Your mother would be proud of you.'

Evie's dad was watching from the doorway. 'Yes, she certainly would.'

He had shaved his beard and when Evie looked at him it was almost like she was looking at him for the first time. He seemed happy. Properly happy, this time. As if he was free. 'Oh, by the way, Evie, I think Beak and his friends have eaten all the seeds. I got some more of his favourite ones from the shop . . .'

Evie smiled gratefully. 'Thanks, Dad. And I've been thinking . . .'

'What about?'

'Names,' Evie told him. 'I mean, Navarro is a better name than Trench, isn't it? Trench sounds a bit like something you get stuck in. And we're not stuck any more. Maybe we should become Navarros again. I'd stay being Evie. Because that fits me. And Eva was always part of my name anyway. But Evie Navarro — what do you reckon? Do you think Mum would like that?'

'The Navarros,' said Evie's dad. He was smiling. But a little tear glistened in his eye. A sad-happy tear. 'And from now on, no more hiding. I will be Santiago again. I like that. I can be the man your mother fell in love with again. I will be your father again. Your true father. With no secrets. I will not lock myself away any more . . .'

'Does that include Mum? Will you tell me everything about her? Everything you remember?'

'Nothing would make me happier,' he told her. 'Nothing at all.'

'I love you, Dad,' said Evie. She hugged him. He hugged her back.

'I love you, too. And from now on, you must never be afraid to be special. It's your gift . . .'

★

After dinner, Evie stroked Scruff, who had just woken up.

'Life is good, Evie,' said Scruff, wagging his tail. 'Life is good.'

And this time she really could agree.

'Yes, Scruff,' said Evie, smiling down at her friend. 'You are right. It really is. Life is good.'

Acknowledgements

Firstly, I must mention Emily Gravett. She was my top choice of illustrator, and it has been incredible seeing how she has brought all the animals (including the human ones) to life.

A big thank you to my agent Clare Conville and all the team at Curtis Brown.

Another big thank you to my editor Francis Bickmore and everyone at Canongate.

And to my first reader, adviser and best friend, Andrea Semple.

I also must mention my daughter Pearl. She asked me to write a book about animals, and a girl who loves them, so I did so just for her. After writing *A Boy Called Christmas* because my son asked me a question ('What was Father Christmas like as a boy?') I needed to keep things even and write a book for Pearl. Here it is!

Finally, I want to acknowledge all the young people everywhere who are determined to protect humans and other animals, and the

243

environment we all inhabit. Greta Thunberg and young climate change activists around the world, I salute you. You are Evie's heroes.

HOW TO MAKE
FAT CAKES
FOR
WILD BIRDS

When it's cold, it can be hard for birds to find enough food to eat. You can help by making them some tasty fat cake treats full of things they love to eat. Hang them outside your window or in your garden and you will be able to see the birds enjoying the yummy snacks you have made.

You will need a saucepan, a large spoon and some clean yoghurt pots, remembering that the bigger your yoghurt pots, the more ingredients you will need.

You will also need some string to hang your fat cakes. Ask an adult to cut you some pieces of string that are long enough to hang your yoghurt pots up with. If you don't have anywhere to hang your fat cakes, leave the string off and put your fat cakes on a flat surface outside, out of reach of other animals and small children, e.g. on a windowsill or bird table.

Makes three fat cakes

INGREDIENTS:

1 yoghurt pot of
vegetable suet
(or beef suet / lard
if you can't find it)

1 yoghurt pot of
bird seed

1 yoghurt pot
mix of sultanas,
unsalted nuts
and oats

METHOD:

1. Ask an adult to help you make a hole in
the bottom of your yoghurt pots
2. Thread your string through each hole, pulling
the string through so it comes out of the top
of each pot, then set them to one side
3. Put the suet or lard into a saucepan and heat
gently until melted, asking an adult to help
4. Take the saucepan off the heat and mix
in the dry ingredients
5. Once the mix has cooled a little and is
safe to handle, pour it into the prepared
yoghurt pots
6. Firmly press the mixture into the yoghurt
pots, making sure the string is in the centre
of the pot once the mix is in
7. Pop the yoghurt pots into the freezer
to set
8. Once set hard, take the pots out of the
freezer and carefully pull each yoghurt pot away.
You can then ask an adult to cut the yoghurt
pot away from the string
9. Tie the two ends of the string together
and hang your fat cakes!

DARE
to be
YOU!

Evie and the
ANIMALS

True or False Animal Facts!

Circle your answers below . . .

1. Sea horses are the only
   animal where the males
   bear the unborn young
   True or False?

2. The more stripes tigers
   have, the more dangerous
   they are
   True or False?

3. Polar bears have black skin
   underneath their fur
   True or False?

4. Flamingos are born pink
   True or False?

5. Spiders can fly
   True or False?

6. Elephants can smell
   water from many
   miles away
   True or False?

7. All octopus have eight
   tentacles, sixteen brains
   and thirty-two eyes
   True or False?

8. The whale shark is the
   largest fish in the sea
   True or False?

9. Dogs ears grow bigger as
   they get older
   True or False?

10. Oysters can change gender
    True or False?

1T / 2F / 3T / 4F / 5F / 6T / 7F / 8T / 9F / 10T

MORE FROM

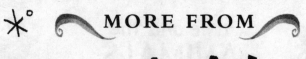

Matt Haig

For all the latest news from Matt Haig and to read more about his books, go to kids.matthaig.com